Praise for Melissa Clark

Praise for *Bear Witness*

"A portrait of heartbreak and resilience, and what happens to those left behind . . . a devastatingly good read."
— Laura Fitzgerald, national bestselling author of *Veil of Roses* and *Dreaming in English*

"Melissa Clark's *Bear Witness* takes a piercing look at the world of Paige Bellen, a young woman whose transition into adolescence is haunted by the kidnapping and death of her best friend: 'One minute everything was normal and then a door opened and it was never the same.' A harrowing, resonant portrait of girlhood trauma."
— Rigoberto González, author of *Butterfly Boy* and *The Mariposa Club*

"Melissa Clark has crafted a perceptive and highly compelling story of a teenage girl, in the wake of a terrible trauma. It is an intense and emotional read, one that left me breathless. *Bear Witness* is a unique combination of page-turner and astutely worded character observation."
— Alan Lazar, author of *Roam*

"A glimpse inside an experience we all would hope never to have to explore. Melissa Clark has told a powerful story."
— Davida Wills Hurwin, author of *A Time for Dancing* and *Freaks and Revelations*

Praise for *Swimming Upstream, Slowly*

"Melissa Clark starts with an idea so convincingly scary it's amazing she can play it out in such a funny, moving, and sexy way. But, boy, does she ever."
— Alan Alda, bestselling author of *Never Have Your Dog Stuffed* and *Things I Overheard While Talking to Myself*

"An absolutely delightful tale of dealing with life's hilarious curve balls. It's smart and snappy, with a hoot of a premise. . . . I loved this book and simply could not put it down!"
— Jennifer Coburn, author of *Reinventing Mona* and *Tales from the Crib*

"A brilliant idea for a book, and a compelling, warm, and funny read."
— Jane Moore, bestselling author of *Fourplay* and *The Second Wives Club*

"Funny, lucid, and sharp-witted, Melissa Clark's nimble first novel is both clever and wise. This up-to-date romantic adventure with a twist is presented with flair, charm, and a keen confident eye for how we live now."
— Les Plesko, author of *The Last Bongo Sunset*

Praise for *Imperfect*

"A perrrfect comedy for those who feel slightly out of place in the world. A touching and witty page-turner."
— Jennifer Coburn, author of *The Wife of Reilly*

"Clark has a unique talent for cleverly conjuring the physical manifestations of human emotions."
— Max Brooks, New York Times bestselling author of *World War Z*

"Unusual, unputdownable, unforgettable."
— Lauren Baratz-Logsted, author of *The Bro-Magnet* and *Z: A Novel*

"A compelling story, told with compassion and intelligence, about two women struggling towards self-acceptance and coming to realize that 'imperfection' is in the eye of the beholder."
— Kathy McCullough, author of *Don't Expect Magic*

Bear Witness

Melissa Clark

SparkPress, a BookSparks imprint
A Division of SparkPoint Studio, LLC

Published by SparkPress, a BookSparks imprint,
A division of SparkPoint Studio, LLC
Tempe, Arizona, USA, 85281
www.sparkpointstudio.com

ISBN: 978-1-940716-75-6 (pbk)
ISBN: 978-1-940716-74-9 (e-bk)

Cover design © Julie Metz, Ltd./metzdesign.com
Cover photo © Getty Images
Author photo © Kevin Salter
Formatting by Polgarus Studio

"We can't return, we can only look behind from where we came, and go round and round and round in the circle game."

— *Joni Mitchell, "Circle Game"*

Tenth Grade

Countless people suggested that Paige focus on something, anything but the crime. It had been volleyball for a little while and before that chorus. Lately, though, her concentration was on grades because good grades meant a good college and a good college ensured a good future. And it was so important for Paige to focus on her future, at least that's what she'd been told by countless other people—Dr. Swick, for instance with his compassionate eyes, and her grandpa Joseph, and Evelyn Davis, the well-meaning counselor at school.

Paige had two years until she'd be able to apply to colleges herself, but watching her sister, Erin, compile her grades and letters of recommendation and lists of extracurricular activities made her realize one could never start too early. Paige observed as Erin pored through a myriad of college books, selecting her favorite choices. She learned about the importance of the "safety" school, the one you might not be dying to attend but that you were practically guaranteed entry into. For Erin, that was UC Santa Barbara. Paige couldn't imagine Erin living anywhere but their house and the thought of her sister moving to Santa Barbara left her with a thick knot in her stomach, but the other choices were worse. Erin was applying to colleges in Vermont, Maine, Massachusetts, and New Hampshire. Why would she want to be so far away? What was so wrong with Northern California? There were plenty of colleges near them, for instance Stanford down in Palo Alto, or Berkeley, which was even closer.

Her sister Erin's bedroom was straight out of a catalogue. Her books, CDs, and DVDs were stored alphabetically on shelves; she had separate bins for library books and even a system in place for due dates.

Paige walked into the room and found the shelf dedicated to Erin's college endeavor. *Getting In Without Freaking Out, Admission Matters, The Ultimate Guide to America's Best Colleges.* Paige reached for the encyclopedia of colleges and when she did, two folded papers slipped out and on to the floor. Leaning down to retrieve them, Paige caught a glimpse of Erin's handwriting, even and precise. She stood, thick college book in one hand, two frayed notebook pages in the other.

"In 1997 I said good-bye to my little sister as she headed to a slumber party at her friend's house. Never in a million years did it cross my mind that I might not see her again. That friend was Robin Hecht, the girl kidnapped in her own home and found

murdered two weeks later. The night my parents received the phone call, all our lives changed in an instant."

Hands trembling, Paige read it again and then a third time. There was more, two pages full, but Paige couldn't get past the first paragraph. Suddenly she was in Robin's room on Golden Lane jumping on Robin's trundle bed. Was she midair when the intruder arrived, hair like a skunk, burly, and breathing hard? *Erin's* life was shattered? *Erin* now claimed the crime as hers?

Paige sat on the bed as a wave of dizziness swept over her. She tucked the papers back into the college book. Surely Erin's story would impress the acceptance committee. How many people could write a firsthand account of the heinous crime? Certainly Erin had known Robin, it was a true relationship, not imagined like all the people who'd been interviewed for the newspapers and on television—the student at Miller Junior High whom Paige had never even seen who claimed Robin as one of her best friends, or the guy at the burger place who remembered serving Robin, the cute girl with the dimple. With Robin's departure came a slew of people filling the void with chatter, a few were familiar to Paige, but most of their relationships were as anecdotal as their stories. What was the need in human nature to stake one's claim in tragedy? What Paige would have given not to be connected, not to be in the inner circle, not to have borne witness to the crime of the decade.

"Paigey," her mom called, knocking her out of her thoughts, "can you come down here for a minute?"

Paige shoved the book back on the shelf where she found it and headed out of Erin's room to the top of the staircase. She shouted down, "What?"

"Come," her mom called. "I want to show you something."

Paige sighed. She hated when people insisted you twist your schedule to fit their needs. She took the stairs two at a time.

"Shh," her mom said. "Come quietly." In the living room, she pointed to the sofa where Lucy and Desi, the two cats, were splayed out and locked in an embrace licking each other. A smile as wide as Texas stretched across her mom's face. "Is that not the cutest thing you've ever seen?" she said. "I mean, tell me that's not the—"

"Adorable," Paige said. "What did you want to show me?"

Her mom looked taken aback. "That!" she said.

"They do that all the time," Paige said.

"I've *never* seen it," her mom insisted.

"Doesn't mean they don't." Paige twirled on her heels and headed back up the stairs.

Her therapist had told her to shout "Stop" whenever she felt her mind start to slide back to that night and loop around the what if's. Paige found herself belching "Stop!" at an alarming rate, like a strange form of Tourette's syndrome. "Stop!" she said out loud once as her mom was preparing dinner—the knife she was using for chopping a cucumber suddenly reminded her of the knife the intruder used to threaten her. "Stop!" she yelled again while she and Erin were watching TV and a commercial for a board game came on, the one the girls had been playing twenty minutes before the intruder arrived. "Stop!" she yelled as she was brushing her teeth one night. What did Paige see in the mirror behind her? A shadow? Or another criminal, poised and ready to pounce?

Back upstairs in the bathroom, Paige sat on the toilet and gazed down between her legs at the water. She'd been on watch for her period since she was twelve. She was embarrassed that at fifteen she was still waiting for that first drop of blood to signify her official arrival into adulthood. All of her friends had gotten it already, some even as early as ten. In ninth grade she'd paid a humiliating visit to the doctor with her mom, where they discussed menstruation as a threesome. It was possible, the doctor told them, that the trauma had delayed it. The stress around the incident as well as the stress around the trial earlier that year was significant. But it was also probable, she'd said, that Paige's active involvement in sports might also be playing a role. Paige's mom explained to the doctor how Erin started hers merely days after her thirteenth birthday, as had she (information Paige didn't really care to hear), and it was worrisome that Paige was so delayed. "Everyone's different," the doctor assured them. Paige nodded, relieved but cold wearing only a paper gown.

She shook away the memory, flushed, and headed back into her room.

When Paige was tired of thinking, her mind flippity-flopping like a fish out of water, she anesthetized herself with television. Most everything worked, from cartoons to cooking shows, PBS to Pay-Per-View. When the television spoon-fed all the entertainment, Paige could let go and get lost, learn the fixings of a croque monsieur or giggle at the latest *Friends* episode.

She was at the edge of the stairs about to go down again to watch something when Erin ran into the house, slamming the front door behind her. Desi and Lucy both scurried out of the living room. "It's freezing," Erin called. It had been an unusually cold fall. Paige took the steps two at a time, joining Erin in the kitchen.

"It's freezing," Erin said again. She was putting the orange kettle on the stove. "Do you want tea?" she asked.

"No, thanks," Paige said, and leaned against the door.

Erin had come from track and she was in shorts and a blue hoodie. Her long, brown hair was pulled into a ponytail; her cheeks were ruddy from the air. Erin was built like an athlete with strong legs and firm arms. If it wasn't track, it was soccer or swimming or softball. Erin loved competing and playing, and had since she was a child.

Despite their two-year age difference, everyone thought they were twins, and while they did have the same olive coloring and wore their brown hair the same long length, Erin was sturdier, more muscular, while Paige was lean and long-limbed.

Erin flipped through a tin canister of tea bags, like she was sorting through a Rolodex file. "Apricot or licorice?" she said, weighing the options out loud. Erin glowed with good health, Paige thought, even the whites of her eyes shone. "Apricot," Erin said, plucking the orange bag and tearing it open. "So what's up?" she said without looking at her sister. "Are you sure you don't want tea?"

"No, thanks," Paige said again.

Once the kettle whistled, Erin lifted it off the stove and poured the hot water into her mug. "Heat, heat," she said as the steam formed and evaporated into thin air.

"How are you going to go to college back East if you can't stand a little cold?" Paige asked, pointedly.

Erin looked at her as she dunked the tea bag into the mug. "Let's see where I get in first," she said.

"But seriously," Paige said, "you won't be able to live in Massachusetts or Vermont."

Erin didn't answer and instead blew into the tea before taking a protracted sip.

"It can be minus thirty something in Vermont, you know," Paige added. She'd recently looked it up online.

Erin set the mug down hard on the counter. Some water splashed out. "Can you stop stressing me out?" she said.

"Stressing *you* out?" Paige said. She could feel herself going from zero-to-one hundred, a familiar trajectory.

"Mom!" Erin called.

"Why do you need Mom?" Paige shot back.

"Because you're being—"

"What?" Paige said, picturing Erin's essay upstairs in that book, slammed between the pages. This was all brewing because of that.

"*Unreasonable*," Erin answered, taking her tea and walking out of the kitchen.

Paige followed her down the hall and into the den. "Mom!" Erin called again.

"Y'know what's *unreasonable?*" Paige started. She didn't want to go there, but she felt she had no choice. It was like the train had already left the station as soon as Erin walked into the house.

"Paige, I'm cold and I'm tired and I'm just not in the mood to engage."

"You're cold and tired?" Paige asked in a condescending baby voice. She was a boxer, now, ready for the fight. "And you need your mommy?"

Erin had called for her twice but there was not even a peep from upstairs. Paige wasn't entirely sure her mom was even home. Perhaps she'd ducked out to the market or to fill up the car. Erin pointed the clicker toward the television and it blinked on. A news show was discussing the White House.

Paige spoke above it. "I saw your essay. The rough draft. The one about Robin," she said.

Erin clicked the TV off. "Why did you see it?" she asked. "Where did you see it?"

"It's not enough that I saw it?" Paige said.

"No," Erin said. "It means either you were on my computer or in my drawer."

"Neither," Paige said. "I was looking at college books and it slipped out."

Erin raised an eyebrow.

"It did," Paige insisted.

"It's not your room anymore. Remember?"

Paige shrugged.

"Anyway, it's not *about* Robin," Erin said, setting her tea down. "Ultimately, it's about me and *my* reaction and experiences."

Paige shrugged again. Silence enveloped the room far longer than was comfortable.

"I'm not the enemy, Paige," Erin finally said.

Paige thought that on that balmy October night three years ago, the stranger stole not only Robin, but destroyed a slew of other relationships, once solid, now fragile and frayed. The fact that Erin hadn't been there, wasn't haunted by nightmares, daymares, and an incessant hum of evil memories was enough to divide them in ways Paige couldn't quite articulate. Erin was seventeen, applying for colleges, and strategizing about her prom date. Her life was affected, of course affected, how could it not be? But to use the tragedy as a way in to a competitive college? A springboard to a future life? Well, Paige simply didn't have the luxury to deconstruct the evening and its aftermath into a thesis statement and supporting paragraphs. It was still a jumble in her mind, a gray mess following her everywhere like Pig-Pen's dirt cloud.

How could she explain to Erin that she *was* the enemy, one of many? Anyone who hadn't been there that night had turned into the enemy—her own parents, her well-meaning friends, relatives in other parts of the country.

Caroline was the only one who could never be the enemy. Caroline who squirmed her way out from her bound hands and feet that night and untied Paige before running down the hall to announce to Robin's sleeping mother that Robin was gone—that a big, burly man had taken her. Robin's mother, roused from sleep, confused, concerned, and then frantic as she raced through the house calling for Robin and then dialing 411 instead of 911, her face screwing up as she repeated, "Information?" before realizing she had misdialed.

Paige's relationship with Caroline was the only relationship that mattered, that was sacred, but even that was tenuous, as Caroline's parents had pulled her out of school and taken her to France to live for a year away from the media glare. They stayed on another year and then another. She sent letters assuring Paige she'd be back junior year and begged her to come visit, but a trip to Paris wasn't in the cards. Paige's parents hardly let her leave the house, let alone the country.

It was as though everything was taken on the same night as Robin. There was innocence, of course, and the hard truth that evil could penetrate walls and show up unannounced in a child's bedroom on a warm October night.

Paige heard the key in the front door. "Hi," her mom called. "Can someone come help me?"

Both Paige and Erin dashed to the front hallway where her mom was loaded down with boxes.

"It's almost the last of it," she said. "I promise. These go in the kitchen and these can stay in the hall until I figure out what to do with them."

"eBay," Paige said.

Erin rolled her eyes, grabbed a box, and dragged it into the kitchen.

Paige was in fifth grade when her mom opened Infinitea. It was a small property on Cyprus wedged between a few antique stores. It started out as just a tea shop—selling exotic and fruit-flavored loose-leaf teas packaged in brown bags—but as word spread and people started coming, she added a few tables and started selling food, as well as tea paraphernalia—strainers, teapots, and cozies. Paige had her eleventh birthday party there—girls only—and they sipped tea and ate cake. Soon other kids started having their parties there as did their parents, and when Infinitea was featured in the *San Francisco Chronicle* people stopped in as they traveled through town—on their way to Tahoe or on their way down South.

Infinitea was in business a little over a year when the crime occurred. At first it opened its doors to volunteers searching for Robin, then it catered to volunteer call centers. Paige's mom reduced her work hours, but the store stayed open for another three years until she realized she was putting more money into her business than she was earning. There were bills to pay now where there hadn't been before, like Dr. Swick's bill, which came once a month for the past three and a half years. While insurance had covered some of it, Paige's parents still had to cover the rest. There was no public assistance program aiding in victim recovery. And then there was Erin's pending college tuition, another four-year expense her parents would have to endure. So, Infinitea finally closed earlier that week. Her mom's dream realized and then, suddenly, vanished.

"I hate Erin," Paige said, and immediately burst into tears. Of course she didn't *hate* Erin, but she was so pissed about that essay. She didn't mean to get so upset. She knew her mother had her own sadness to bear.

"What happened?" her mom said, concerned. Paige was pulling a box into the hallway but her mom made her stop. "What happened?" she said again.

Paige couldn't stop crying now and when Erin showed up back in the hallway she said, "What's going on?"

"That's what I'm trying to figure out," her mom said.

"Is this about the essay?" Erin said, snappish, which only made Paige feel worse. "She was in my room, rummaging through my stuff . . . ," Erin told her mom.

"I was looking at college books," Paige wailed.

"And she says one of my essays slipped out."

"It did!"

"The one about Robin."

Their mom stood next to Paige, rubbing her back.

"I didn't ask her to go into my room and rifle through—"

Her mom covered her own lips with a finger. Paige couldn't see because she was now kneeling over the box, her tears making tapping sounds as they fell, temporarily staining the cardboard.

"I did nothing wrong," Erin said, defiantly, and soon she, too, was filled with tears. "I'm so tired of walking on eggshells."

Paige thought, *walking on eggshells?*

Their mom set her purse down and took each girl under her arms, stroking their hair, because there simply weren't anymore words left to say.

Crime had touched their family once before. When Paige was seven, her parents took a trip to Europe, visiting three countries in twelve days. Paige and Erin stayed home, their grandparents flew in from Denver to watch them. One morning while they were having breakfast, the phone rang and Paige's grandma picked up. Her normal "Hello" morphed quickly to "No!" and then, "Oh, goodness!" When she covered her mouth, Paige knew something was really wrong.

"Can I talk?" she asked her grandma, reaching for the phone.

But her grandmother held up her hand, silently telling her to wait. "No!" she said again into the phone. "Is he okay?"

Paige was twitchy, eager to hear what had happened.

"Of course!" her grandmother said. "He could have had a knife. Or a gun!"

Paige's heart was racing. She knew it was her mother on the other line, but what had happened? Was her dad okay?

She eventually heard the story.

Her parents had been in Barcelona, strolling through a park when a man walked by and spattered paint on her dad's jacket and ran off. Another man ran over and started to wipe it off. "Thank you so much," her mom said. But in the blink of an eye that man ran off, too, taking with him her dad's camera and his wallet, which was nestled in his back pocket. It had been a perfect tag-team crime.

Her parents talked about it for weeks after their return and although Paige was too young to comprehend the nuances of the story, she was aware of how many times her parents recounted it—to each other at the dinner table and to their friends over the phone. They spoke of "schemes" and "scams" and "desperate crazies," and Paige started coming to the conclusion that Europe was not a place she'd like to visit, ever.

Paige dashed back upstairs and in the bathroom threw water on her tear-streaked face. She could hear murmurs from downstairs between her mom and sister but she couldn't hear the details. She shut the door between the bathroom and Erin's room, and then shut the door between her own room and the bathroom. And finally, she slammed the door to her room, making sure everyone in the house could hear it. Dinner would be in an hour but she already knew she wouldn't be hungry and that would turn into another *thing*.

At her desk, Paige picked up a recent postcard from Caroline. The letters between them had gone from thick, colorful piles to mere postcards ever since the trial last year. They'd promised to write when Caroline first left for Paris and they'd spent that first summer away from each other poring out their souls on paper. Dr. Swick had referred to them as "battle buddies," having endured a war together. Caroline's parents weren't like Paige's. They didn't believe in therapy. Shortly after the incident, Caroline attended a few months worth of sessions with her own doctor, but then that was that, and by the summer she was out of the country.

The most recent postcard was a picture of a fountain in the Jardin du Luxembourg. On the other side Caroline had scrawled:

Paging Paige,
Spent the day at the Luxembourg Garden with JC. We had a picnic of bread and cheese (of course) and walked around smelling roses. Miss you. Bisou, bisou!

Love,
Sweet Caroline

Her news came in sound bites now, and lately revolved around her new boyfriend, Jean-Christophe. Paige's jealousy was palpable every time she read about him. Paige was still in school with Gus, Benjamin, and Bruce, and had been with most of them since elementary school. The most exotic guy was an exchange student from Spain named Devlin, but he was immediately snatched up by Ashleigh before Paige even had a chance to crush on him. And there was Caroline, living it up in Paris with her boyfriend, gardens, and lots of cheese and bread.

Paige opened the middle desk drawer and glanced at the white envelope at the top of the pile. Two years later and she still didn't know if she should mail it. It's not as though the letter took up any space, but it was a constant reminder of things left unsaid. She slipped Caroline's postcard underneath the pile and slammed the drawer shut.

Paige was startled by a knock on her door. "What?" she hissed.

"Can I come in?" It was Erin.

"No," Paige said.

An hour later Paige's mom knocked.

"What?" Paige said.

"Dinner."

"I'm not hungry."

"Paige," her mom said, "you have to eat."

"Don't worry about it."

A few minutes later her dad knocked.

"What?" Paige said.

"You're not joining us for dinner?" he said in a sweet, hurt tone.

"No, thanks," she said.

"May I come in?" he asked.

"Not really," she said. Tears were starting to form again. She couldn't help feeling angry toward everyone. Her mom and dad had done nothing wrong but she couldn't stand the thought of sitting around the dinner table watching everyone try to cheer her up. It would be easier on the whole family if she just stayed in her room.

"Okay," her dad said. "I'll bring your dinner up later."

Paige plucked the stuffed animal bear out of the basket at the foot of her bed and squeezed him tight. Cinnamon was less the color of the spice and more the color of gingerbread. He was a medium-sized bear, paws outstretched. His eyes were black beads and his smile, a few stitches of thick, red thread, was simple and comforting. He lived in a wicker basket with other stuffed animals by the foot of her bed. She had, once upon a time, a strong relationship with the other animals—a little black dog she named "Ralph," a soft owl, a few bears of her own. She used to line them up against the window ledge and weave fictional narratives, owl running for president, Ralph and a girl bear getting married, but now they lived in a clump. Every now and then, though, she rearranged the animals so that Cinnamon was at the top of the heap, not at the bottom suffocating.

Sometimes Paige fantasized about giving him away. He was with her because he wasn't with Robin. Would Paige have to keep him until twelfth grade? Drag him to college, wherever she went? What about after college? Would Cinnamon follow her the rest of her life? Another child might love these animals, she sometimes told herself. A child in need would know only joy when playing with Cinnamon, not the pain that Paige felt every time, every single time, she looked at the bear. Cinnamon could be part of a new stuffed-animal universe. Perhaps by releasing him, she could release herself, too. Wouldn't it be the right thing to do for both of them? She put her head on the bear's belly, using it as a pillow, but it wasn't comfortable. She wasn't comfortable.

"Stop!" she commanded herself. It had been a few months since her mind had wandered like this. She stared out the window. "Stop!" she said again. She faced the street, lampposts, rooftops, and second-story windows. "Stop," she said quietly, almost begging.

Later that evening, after what must have been an hour, lying on her bed staring at the ceiling, Paige answered her dad's knock and took the tray of food to her desk. It was like room service, only this waiter folded her in his arms and hugged her, without words or platitudes, and she ate two fish tacos—her favorite—not realizing how hungry she'd really been.

At school the next day, Paige walked down the hallway toward her locker. Up ahead she could see Ashleigh handing out fliers, a commotion surrounding her, as usual. Paige's first instinct was to run the other way—it always seemed to be her first instinct. She feared it was another social event, and while her friends were always so kind about inviting her here and there, Paige found that she felt calmer, better, safer at home in front of the television.

"Paigey!" Ashleigh called when she saw her. She waved a flier in front of her. "I will be personally insulted if you don't come," she said.

Paige took the paper and kept walking. "Late for class," she lied. When she got to her locker she glanced at it. It was a Xeroxed image of Ashleigh as a child, dressed as a pumpkin. *Think Halloween is just for kids? Join me, Saturday, October 31 to find out!* What did that even mean? Of course Halloween was for kids.

Halloween had been Paige's favorite holiday—more than Christmas, more than Easter, more than her birthday, even—until "the incident." Halloween now had a sinister meaning. Ghosts weren't just cute white things, but shadows of people who had passed. Simply put, Paige found it unnecessary to flirt with fear ever since a hulking, bearded man nearly frightened her to death.

In fact, a few days after Robin was taken, Paige and her family drove downtown to police headquarters to meet with a criminal sketch artist. Looking out the window of the backseat of her parents' car, Paige saw pumpkins sitting on porches, skeletons dangling from doorways. Halloween was just five days away. The neighborhoods were decorated in death—ghosts blew in the winds, silhouettes of black cats arched in fear sat on stoops. There was less than a week until the decorations came down, the pumpkins got tossed, and people made way for Thanksgiving. Halloween would be tucked away until next year, but Paige's nightmare was just beginning. She, Robin, and Caroline were going to dress as genies that year, but with Robin still missing, Paige wanted nothing to do with trick or treating. Fuck candy. All she wanted was Robin. Was it possible she was behind one of those doors? Could Paige ring every bell in the neighborhood under the guise of a genie looking for candy, when really she was just Paige Bellen looking for her best friend?

In science they were studying geology. Mr. Kholos was giving a lecture on volcanoes, how the heat below caused fissures above, breaks in the earth, earth that had been bound together for hundreds of thousands of years. "Volcanoes are nature's way of cooling off the planet, and releasing internal heat and pressure," he said. Paige took notes and drew volcanoes in the margins of her paper, lava squiggles dripping down the sides.

Paige had always been a good student, a "gifted" student, placed in an after-school reading-enrichment program in fourth grade and the advanced math section in sixth. Seventh grade started out hopeful with A's on quizzes and essays, but as expected, after Robin's disappearance, Paige had little to no ability to concentrate on schoolwork. Teachers made concessions, tutors were hired, but Paige went through a long phase where she simply didn't see the point of any of it. In the beginning when she went to Dr. Swick twice a week, he helped her with concentration tips, explained the importance of the routine of school in her recovery.

Now that Paige was observing Erin go through the college process she was able to snap back into student mode.

Her grades slowly climbed back up, past the C's of late and on toward B plusses and even A's. And at her first consultation with Evelyn Davis, the college counselor, she was relieved to hear that the climb in grades could actually be more effective than steady grades, and what with her background any admissions committee was going to look at the bigger picture, take everything into consideration.

At the end of science class, Mr. Kholos reminded them of their test next week and Paige wrote it down again in her notebook: science exam 11/3 because without constant reminders she was still likely to forget.

Paige sat on the couch and waited as Dr. Swick fiddled with the temperature gauge on the wall. He did this every week for the past three years. When he finally took his seat across from her she said, "My sister's writing about the kidnapping for her college entry essay."

Swick nodded. "How do you feel about that?"

She knew he knew how she felt—he just always had to ask those questions. Paige shrugged. "Whatever works," she said.

"What do you mean by that?" Dr. Swick shrugged back.

"An essay like that's going to make her stand out in a crowd," she said. "She's going to get into a good college because of it."

"That's wonderful," he said. "Don't you want your sister to get into a great college?"

"Yeah, but not based on my experience."

"Paige," he said. "I want to point out that this is the first time you've ever referred to it as 'the kidnapping.'"

She shifted on the couch, trying to remember if that was true.

"In the past, you've always called it 'the incident,'" he said.

Paige nodded. Yes, he was right about that.

"We can't control or measure how the trauma affected other people," he said. And then, "I know you know, because we've talked about it before."

Paige nodded again.

"When President Kennedy was shot, people all over the world experienced grief; probably people who didn't even vote for him. Same with John Lennon, Princess Diana. The grief around their deaths was real."

"But I *found* the essay," Paige said. "She wasn't even going to show it to me."

"You don't know that," he said.

"I'm pretty sure I'm right. I know my sister."

Paige explained the circumstances. The papers in the college book, how they slipped out so innocently and practically smacked her across the face with their contents.

"You know what I think?" Dr. Swick said. "I think you were caught off guard, and that's what's so upsetting to you."

"I don't know," Paige said.

"It hasn't been part of your daily dialogue," he said, "like it was in the beginning. And then all of a sudden—"

When she thought about it, she thought he could be right. Even in therapy they'd been talking about other things lately, her mom, for starters, her geometry class, in which she was still struggling.

"Your family experienced trauma, too," Dr. Swick said. "It's probably one of the most significant things—if not *the* most significant—that happened in your sister's life. Right?" Before Paige could answer he said, "You know, there was an experiment. Have I told you this? The monkeys?"

Paige never remembered discussing monkeys in therapy.

"Well, there was a famous experiment done in the late fifties where they had two monkeys, one received electric shocks every few minutes while the other watched. At the end of the experiment they measured both monkeys' stress levels, and guess who experienced *significantly* more stress?"

He answered before Paige could even begin to figure it out.

"The monkey *watching*," he said. "The observer."

The observer. Paige thought that Swick was trying to make the point that Erin was the observer in this case, but wasn't it Paige who observed her best friend get carried out of her own home on a stranger's shoulder? Paige quickly realized that it wasn't a competition over whose stress levels were higher. Everyone felt stress when Robin disappeared, from the mailman to Robin's teachers, everyone with a heartbeat was glued together with stress.

"It's going to be so weird when Erin goes to college," she said, softening. "She's never <u>not</u> been in the room next to me, except for when she went to camp."

Swick smiled warmly. "It's going to be an adjustment," he agreed. "But we'll cross that bridge when we get there."

She'd crossed so many already but there were still so many to come.

"It's all part of growing up," Swick said as he wrote out a bill for her to bring home to her parents.

In the months following the incident, Paige developed a series of unfortunate tics. They drove her mom and sister crazy, and quite frankly she couldn't stand them either, but nor could she stop herself. The tics included tooth scraping, with the nail of her right thumb, which she wedged along the gum line and between teeth—all thirty of them. It probably looked to most like she was biting her nail. When she finished scraping, sometimes collecting plaque and food particles under her nail, she'd run her tongue around and around her mouth, feeling for any irregularities. Then there was the hair splitting. She'd examine each singular strand for split ends and when she found one she'd tear it off. Another habit included counting bites of food as she chewed. No one but she knew about this one as it all took place in her head. The worst was with gum, counting from the second she popped a stick in, to when she spat it out. She tried not to chew too often because there was really very little pleasure in it. Foot tapping. Eyebrow smoothing. This was the one that drove her mother the battiest. "Your eyebrows are going to fall out!" she'd snapped recently at the dinner table. The funny thing was, Paige didn't even realize she was doing it.

Her mom picked her up from therapy at four fifty-five, five minutes late. "I could see you scraping your teeth from a block away," she said. Paige shrugged it off. There were more boxes from the tea shop in the front seat. "I'll move them," her mom said, unbuckling her seat belt.

"It's okay," Paige said, climbing into the backseat.

"I'll move them," her mom said again.

"Don't worry about it," Paige said, settling in. "I want to be in the back."

Her mom looked at her through the rearview mirror. Paige could only see brown eyes and a furrowed brow, a familiar sight.

"How was your sess—"

"Fine."

Her mom put the car in drive and they headed down the street toward the highway. Paige looked out the window at the billowy clouds that dotted the sky. No shapes emerged; they were merely clouds.

"I have the bill," Paige said. "Remind me to give it to you." She peered into her backpack and saw the folded up bill next to the invitation to Ashleigh's party she'd received earlier in the day.

"Okay," her mom said.

They merged onto the highway, the setting sun bright through the car window. Paige held her left hand up to shield her eyes. "Can I go to a party on Halloween?" she asked.

Her mom's eyes popped into view again, only this time her brows were raised. "A party?" she said.

"Ashleigh Gordon," Paige said, anticipating the next question.

"Ashleigh," her mom said in a tone that suggested she was trying to match the name with the face.

"Her parents will be there," Paige assured her, though she wasn't entirely sure that was true.

"Is it dress up?"

"If by 'dress up' you mean 'costume,' then yes," Paige said.

The eyes gazed at her through the mirror now looking hurt.

"Dress up?" Paige repeated. "We're not four."

They drove the rest of the way in silence. Paige wondered what she'd wear to the party. Her mom put on the classical music station but they only caught the end of a movement before the news started. Her mom clicked it off.

When they finally pulled into the driveway, Paige's mom twisted around and said, "You're awfully quiet today. Whatcha thinkin' about back there?"

Paige knew her mom meant well but she just wasn't in the mood to talk to her, couldn't stand the cutesy tone. She shrugged, her poor shoulders always scrunched up toward her ears. "I was just taking in the scenery," she said, which wasn't a complete lie. She unbuckled her seat belt and helped her mom carry the last of the boxes inside the house.

A sea of dates rolled in throughout the year—cresting and crashing over Paige like an aggressive wave. October 24, the day Robin was taken. November 10, the day her remains were found; November 22, the memorial; February 27, Robin's birthday; September 13, the beginning of the trial. Paige couldn't imagine there'd be a time when these dates lost their significance, when October 24 was just another fall day. Dr. Swick explained to her that the body stores memories, too, and that she shouldn't be surprised if she felt ill around those dates. It was common, he said, even expected. It was mid-October now, the days inching closer and closer to another anniversary of the very worst kind. Once, in eighth grade, she literally couldn't get out of bed, only to realize it was a year to the day that Robin was found.

Paige wasn't the only one who experienced somatic symptoms. She was concerned about her dad, too, who now walked hunched over and complained of back pains. Once when she came home from volleyball practice he was flat on his back on the kitchen floor. "I'm okay, back just went," he said in a strained voice. Paige reached her hand out to try and help him up but he said, "No, it feels good like this." More recently, early before school she found him on the floor next to his side of the bed as she dashed in to get a spritz of her mom's perfume. She thought he'd fallen. "Dad!" she said, alarmed, but then realized he had a pillow under his head and seemed somewhat comfortable. "He likes it down there," her mom said, her eyes still shut and her voice early-morning raspy.

Up in her room, Paige dumped the contents of her backpack onto her bed. She had piles of homework to accomplish but she wasn't in the mood. Instead, she sat at her desk and started a letter to Caroline but stopped when she realized she'd have more to write after Ashleigh's Halloween party, plus she was out of stamps. She put the stationery back inside the middle drawer. That other white envelope, addressed, stamped, and ready to go teased her with its presence. She slammed the drawer shut, grabbed a jacket from her closet, and took the stairs two at a time. "Mom?" she called. "I'm going to run to the post office. Do you need anything?"

Her mom emerged from the kitchen. "I was just going to go to the store," she said. "I'll give you a ride."

"I kind of wanted to walk," Paige said.

Her mom said, "Oh," and Paige felt bad, like she had somehow insulted her.

"Why don't you give me a ride there and I'll walk back."

"Okay," her mom said, cheerfully. "Let me just get my keys."

Paige couldn't wait to get her driver's license next summer when she turned sixteen. She'd drive the red Subaru wagon that Erin drove now. She wondered what rules would come with the car; she hoped not too many because she was eager for a taste of freedom.

In the car her mom said, "I'm dropping the business keys off to the new owners. This is the final good-bye."

Paige pouted in synch with her mom. "One door closes and another opens," Paige said.

"When did you get so wise?" her mom asked.

The drive took less than five minutes.

"I'm walking back," Paige reminded her as she parked.

Her mom's eyebrows knitted into worry.

"Mother," Paige said, cautioning her. She exhaled. "I'll see you at home."

The post office was around the block from Infinitea and Paige went to the left as her mom went to the right. Paige joined the line, staring absentmindedly at the Space Shuttle stamp posters on the wall.

As soon as she saw her she wanted to run the other way, but it was too late; Mrs. Hecht—was that even still her name now that she was divorced?—Robin's mom—had spotted her. Paige thought she looked angry, but then she softened. She'd aged significantly since the time she last saw her at the trial; her eyes looked sunken, almost hollow. Paige wanted nothing more than to turn away. "We're moving," she told Paige as she approached. "I'm just filling out the change-of-address cards."

"Where?" Paige asked, picturing first an empty house, and then one with a new family. She didn't know which image was worse.

Mrs. Hecht brought her pile of cards over to where Paige was now paying for stamps. "Mendocino," she said in a soft voice. "I've always wanted to live there."

Paige had been there once before, visiting her sister at camp, the camp she was hoping to attend the next summer, but never did. Paige nodded. She didn't know what else to do. A thought popped in her mind fleetingly before she defused it with logic. The thought was: what if Robin returns and there's only an empty house, or a new family in it? And then the logic: Robin's not coming back.

"How are you, sweetie?" Mrs. Hecht asked.

How was she? Some days fine. Better than the year before, maybe, but not as good as at the beginning of seventh grade. She was told she had youth on her side, which would allow her more time to heal, whatever that meant. She was getting by. Usually. Right now she was not well. Seeing Robin's mom made her feel unwell. "I'm okay," Paige said. "Thanks." She wondered if anyone else in line knew the players of the conversation. Three years ago they would have known for sure. Paige's picture had been all over the newspapers, and although Robin's dad had been the one most present in the media, her mom had shown up now and then, too, with Robin's face, only older.

The whole town sprang into action when Robin was taken. A call center sprouted up near Infinitea in an empty, first-floor office space. Paige and Caroline and their parents and siblings all volunteered in whatever capacity they could. Teachers, doctors, librarians, lawyers, everyone emerged to help, putting their best foot forward. It was like they were the most motivated team ever, ready to fight the other team: Team Bad Guy, Team Crime. They thought for sure they'd win; they were primed and ready. They faxed descriptions of Robin throughout the country, made signs, took donations, followed leads, checked the Internet, and as the media descended on their small town everyone made sure to hold up a photo of Robin, in the foreground, in the background, it didn't matter as long as her image was seen out there. Paige kept thinking that Robin was going to be so embarrassed about all the attention when she came home. Everything about her was so public now, whereas normally she'd been such a private person. Her dad marched around the media vans, grabbing the news mics and demanding the intruder return his daughter. Paige and her family had moved to a hotel, but other kids had joined with neighboring families and had giant slumber parties, so as not to be alone. The energy was electric, the atmosphere almost like a party, only the reason behind everything was so grave, so impossible to comprehend.

When Robin's body was finally recovered it was like the whole town imploded—falling into itself like a ruined upside-down cake. The media vans eventually drove away, the posters came down, the articles subsided. A memorial service was held for Robin, followed by a somber Thanksgiving and Christmas—everything was off-kilter. But by Easter things on the outside seemed to return to normal— not the old normal with Robin in the world, but the new normal. Paige went to the dentist, did her homework, and called her friends; Erin even celebrated her birthday with a big party at the house. The office space that had temporarily been a call center was leased to a chiropractor. Paige thought that if an alien came to Earth, never in a million years would he think this town, this green, hilly, friendly town, had gone through such a tragedy.

Paige felt that people in the post office were watching and listening to them, and this forced her to speak barely above a whisper. "When are you moving?" she now asked Robin's mom.

"We're pretty much moved already," she said. "I'm just taking care of the particulars."

Paige wondered who the "we" was, wondered if Mrs. Hecht had married the man she'd been dating when Robin was taken. In a way, she didn't want to know.

Paige paid for and received the stamps. She pocketed the change and wondered how long she had to endure this interaction.

"Are you heading out?" she asked Paige, and together they exited the building. "I see your mom's shop closed," she said with a pout.

"Yeah."

"Everything's changing around here," she said.

Paige now had a subject for her letter to Caroline. She wondered how Caroline would have handled this situation. She wanted to tell Mrs. Hecht how much she missed Robin but didn't want to end up crying with her on the steps of the post office. That would be the worst thing ever.

"I hope you love your new home," Paige said after an excruciatingly long silence. She immediately felt stupid. How could she love any home without Robin in it? But then she remembered her mom calling her "wise," just minutes ago in the car, and thought, perhaps, it wasn't the worst thing to say.

"You'll keep in touch?" Robin's mom said.

Paige nodded, though she couldn't fathom how that would work. Still, she didn't rule it out.

Paige walked the six blocks home wondering what the odds were of running into Robin's mom. If she'd walked to the post office, as she'd originally wanted to, she probably would have missed Mrs. Hecht. Fate always seemed to be playing mind games with her, but why? Was there a reason? Or was it just dumb luck? She decided she didn't want to talk about it when she got home, didn't want the worriers to descend on her again. She'd bring it up with Dr. Swick at their next session.

It was easier befriending the new kids, the ones she hadn't known since elementary and middle school. The new ones—Ashleigh, Mary, and Joanna—certainly knew about the crime, but weren't apt to immediately associate Paige with it. The days of slumber parties had ended the night of Robin's. Perhaps Paige would have grown out of them anyway? She wondered what it would be like when Caroline returned from France. She'd missed her so desperately in the beginning, had cried to her parents on multiple evenings wondering why Caroline's parents had to rip her out of the community, leaving Paige as the sole representative of that night.

After considering various costumes, Paige settled on dressing as a baby for Halloween. She'd gone to the drugstore and bought a pacifier and bottle there, and at home put on a pair of tights and made a diaper out of an old, white sheet, fastening it together with two cartoon-sized safety pins she found in her mother's sewing kit. An hour before the party, Erin French braided Paige's hair into two pigtails and her whole family rallied around her downstairs as she revealed the costume.

"Adorable!" her mom said. "Let me get my camera."

Her dad suggested she wear the pacifier around her neck on a ribbon and wedge the bottle into her diaper like a gun in a holster. Everyone laughed when her dad added the final touches and Paige was pleased with her costume, happy to be going to a party. She heard the honking of a car horn outside. Everyone ushered her out the front door and waved to Beth and her mom, who had offered to drive her there.

When she arrived at Ashleigh's house, Paige stood out against the fairies and foxy witches. Debbie Schneider was dressed as a young Madonna in a black-lace bra, mesh shirt, and big hoop earrings. The guys were pirates and sports figures.

"Hi baby," Bruce, as Bill Clinton, said to her.

"Ohmygod!" Ashleigh squealed when she saw her. "You're so cute, Paigey! Ga ga goo goo!"

A cluster of girls circled and acknowledged her and then moved on to the guys. Paige felt like a huge dork, and went into the kitchen to empty her bottle of milk out into the sink.

"You should fill it with vodka," Bruce said, joining her there. "No one would know. Everyone would think it was water."

"Yeah," Paige said weakly.

Bruce started opening cabinets.

"Stop," Paige said. "Her parents are home, you can't—"

"Bingo," Bruce said. A cabinet next to the oven was filled with liquor. Is this what people do at parties now? Paige had been to so few that she really didn't know. Bruce took the bottle from her and swiftly uncapped the vodka, pouring it straight in.

Paige looked around nervously. "You're so bad," she told him. He'd always been this way, ever since she'd known him as a kid, only now it was alcohol and probably drugs when before it had been acting out, back talk, and pranks.

"I'm harmless, Paige. Look, didn't even fill it up halfway." He put the vodka back in the cupboard and attached the nipple back onto the bottle, after taking a swig. "It's like a shot glass," he said, handing it over. Paige squirted a drop into her own mouth and swallowed the sharp taste, like pungent water. She extended her tongue out as though coughing up a fur ball. "Pretty," Bruce said, and she followed him back out into the party.

The living room was a dance floor for the night and hip-hop music was blasting from the speakers. Bruce weaved his way into the crowd and fell easily into the rhythms, moving his hands like he was the DJ scratching the records. There was a man watching from the sidelines. There was something Paige didn't like about him. There were lots of people she didn't recognize.

"Hi, Paige." It was Kaj, someone she definitely knew, dressed in jeans and a black shirt. Paige looked him up and down, trying to figure out what he was. "I'm a concept piece," he explained. "Man versus self." Paige smiled, though she still didn't get it. "I haven't seen you since—"

"Since I was a baby?" Paige said with a laugh. It felt like the vodka was starting to kick in. She took the bottle out from her diaper holster and squeezed another shot into her mouth.

"I was going to say since the trial."

The music was pumping, everyone was dancing, and now Kaj had to go and bring up the trial? "Has it really been that long?" she said.

Kaj nodded. He'd left for private high school after eighth grade and had indeed been at parts of the trial last summer, sometimes in the holding room because the courtroom was so jammed. He'd been there with so many others, pieces of Robin's life who had come together again, in a weak and final attempt at making her whole.

Before the trial, the last time Paige had a conversation with Kaj was on her bed in eighth grade. It was a conversation first between them, and second between their tongues; and all conversations after that were stilted and abrupt.

"The trial," Paige said. What more was there to say about it? Paige brought her bottle to her lips again for one more squirt. "How're you doing?" she asked.

He was standing there looking at her, not really speaking. He shrugged as an answer.

"Yeah?" she said.

"School's good," he said. "Hey, do you still speak to Caroline? Last time I talked to her was—"

"At the trial," they said in unison.

"Yeah," he confirmed. "She seemed really good. I thought it was weird that she moved to Paris, but I guess it was good for her."

The music thumped and Paige started moving with it, bopping her head, shaking her shoulders. "She's in love," Paige said, "with a French guy, of course. She's supposed to move back here next year, but I don't think she will."

Kaj stuck his hands in his pockets. "Oh, wow." He gazed toward the dancing crowd, as did Paige, and they both spotted Ashleigh, who was crouched to the floor and reaching into a back bend, all to the beat of the music.

"She's flexible," Paige said.

Kaj said, "Yeah."

He seemed so bored with the night. Why was he even here? Paige wondered if that's how she came off. She hoped not. "There's vodka in my bottle," she confessed. "Want a sip?"

Kaj pulled a hand out of his pocket and held it out to indicate stop. "No," he said. "I'm fine, thanks. Do you and Caroline ever—"

"I'm going to dance," Paige said and motioned for him to come with her, but again he said, "I'm fine, thanks," and walked away.

Paige shimmied toward Ashleigh and Devlin, Ashleigh's exchange-student boyfriend. "Paigey!" Ash screamed when she saw her, and grabbed her hand, forcing her moves. They ended up slow dancing to the fast music. Paige looked up and saw the man who was standing at the perimeter of the dance floor now hovering over them. She tugged on Ashleigh, who looked behind her. "Hi, Daddy," she said, and Paige instantly relaxed. He said he was going to take the dog for a walk. Ashleigh didn't miss a beat, spinning Paige around like a ballerina and then releasing her into the crowd where Paige bumped and thumped with the rest of the party. It felt good to be moving. People smiled at her. She banged hips with Bruce when she came upon him again. She joined Beth in mouthing the lyrics: "*Don't push me 'cause I'm close to the edge/I'm tryin' not to lose my head/It's like a jungle sometimes it makes me wonder how I keep from going under.*"

For the splitist of seconds, Paige thought she saw fifteen-year-old Robin a few people behind Bruce. Her hair was longer and thicker but she was dancing in that hopping way Robin used to. The feeling of exuberance was so strong and sudden that for an instant Paige's heart raced—her friend was here! Alive and dancing at a party! But then the girl, whoever she was, turned around, and Paige caught the profile, a far cry from Robin's beautiful face. The music, which seconds ago had been loud and enticing suddenly sounded like a funeral dirge. How could everyone be dancing so carefree and sexy when one of their own had been murdered only three years ago? Paige found herself standing in the middle of the dance floor while everyone else was still in motion. Bruce knocked her with his hip again. She stumbled a little to her left and someone jabbed her with an elbow. She needed to get out of there but couldn't find her way off the dance-floor maze. "Excuse me, excuse me!" she said, walking in circles, but nobody seemed to hear her, even as she got louder. She came face-to-face with Not Robin and glared at her for being alive.

Her mind grew cloudy as it jumped from *I have to get out of here* to *I'm going to die, too, eventually.* Finally, she found the sliding glass door that lead to the backyard and she pulled it, but it was stronger than she was. She felt warm, and then hot, like the volcanoes Mr. Kholos had lectured about in school the other day. She pulled again, tears now starting to swim out of her eyes. The third time she tried, it slid open because someone had helped her from behind. "It was locked," Kaj said. Of course it was. That's how criminals were prevented from coming inside. He nudged her outside even though she wasn't entirely sure why she was heading there. He followed her and slid the door shut again so they could only hear the muted thump of the bass line as it pounded from inside. "You're so pale," he told her. "You need to sit." And he guided her to the outdoor seating area where she fell into a yellow patio chair, tears turning to sobs, embarrassed that her first social outing in years had dissolved into this, embarrassed that her internal volcano had erupted.

She was shaking from her toes up. She thought she felt Kaj's arm around her, again, after all this time. "You're okay," he told her.

She said, "No, I'm not," insistently. "I'm not." It felt good to say it. It felt good to finally tell the truth.

Kaj reached into his pocket and pulled out a cell phone. "We should call your parents," he suggested.

"No!" Paige said. Anyone but them. What could they do or say anymore? She was beyond help, out of control, the way her tears were now. Her parents wouldn't be able to fix anything no matter how hard they tried.

Kaj sat still as sorrow emptied out of her, flowing in a way it hadn't ever before. He didn't question her or try to stop the tears. He just sat, in his smart and quiet way, for ten, twenty, thirty minutes until the storm began to pass, until her heaving turned back to breathing.

"You've always been so calm," Kaj said. "I've never understood it."

"Well . . . ," Paige started to say. *Well, not anymore.* Or maybe, *Well, I've been faking it.* Maybe she looked calm from the outside, but that's never how she felt. A volcano was always brewing inside. She couldn't contain it anymore; the pressure was just too much. "Well, maybe I'll call my sister," Paige said when she was able to form words, and Kaj passed her his phone. She took a deep breath and dialed the number of the cell phone her parents had given Erin for emergencies only.

"Erin," she said when her sister picked up, her own party noises in the background, "I need you."

Kaj and Paige were sitting on the front steps of Ashleigh's house when Erin pulled up to the curb in her red Subaru and hopped out of the car.

"You promise you'll tell Beth I got a ride home?" Paige asked, standing.

"Of course," Kaj said. "I'll tell her right now."

"Sorry about all this," Paige said, waving her hand around.

And Kaj said, "I'm happy I could be here for you," which made Paige furrow her brows like her mother. *Happy? To watch me spill my guts out?* "I'll check in on you tomorrow?" he said. "You still have the same number?"

Paige nodded. He put his hand on her back to lead her down the three brick stairs and then turned around to go back into the house.

Erin was still in her Halloween costume, a ladybug. She met Paige at the bottom of the steps. "Are you okay?" She reached out to hug Paige but her antennae headband got caught in Paige's hair.

"Ouch," Paige said.

"Sorry!" Erin said, trying to untangle them.

Paige started laughing.

Erin finally reclaimed her antennae, and they walked to the car. "What's going on?" Erin asked, gazing sadly at her.

Paige didn't know what she looked like, but by Erin's expression it probably wasn't good. She was a big, crying baby. "I don't know," Paige said, stepping into the car. "I think maybe I had too much vodka? I just totally lost it."

"It's okay," Erin said. "You're allowed to lose it." She started the engine. "Vodka?"

"Maybe I didn't have too much," Paige said. "Bruce substituted it for the milk."

"So? Where to?" Erin said.

"I have to do something. I have a letter to mail." Paige said. This was it. The moment had arrived. She felt it in her gut.

"Now?"

"Yeah, but I have to get it first."

Erin kept her eyes on the road. "Get it from where?"

"It's at home, in the middle desk drawer in my room. It's the one on top of the pile. The white envelope. You'll know it when you see it."

"Wait, *I'm* getting it?"

"I can't let Mom and Dad see me like this. I don't want to have to explain. I don't want them to worry."

"Okay," Erin conceded.

They drove home and Erin parked in the driveway and ran inside, leaving the key in the ignition. Paige pulled down the passenger-side visor and looked at herself in the mirror. She looked like a bloated frog, with heavy lids puffed above two slits for eyes.

"Paige!" Erin said, reentering the car.

Paige motioned for her to hand over the letter.

"You're really going to mail this?"

Paige took the envelope, put it on her lap.

"What does it say?" Erin asked, cautiously.

"I don't even remember at this point," Paige said. "I wrote it in eighth grade."

"Are you sure you want—"

"Positive," Paige said.

Erin sighed as she backed out of the driveway and drove around the block looking for a blue postal box.

"Maybe we should go to the official post office," Paige said.

"It's Saturday night," Erin reminded her.

"But I trust it there."

Erin drove the car without any more questions.

It was only nine thirty but by the looks of it trick or treating was over. The neighborhood was still, the pumpkin lights dim. Another Halloween, now the fourth since the crime, had ended.

"I ran into Robin's mom here the other day," Paige said when the car approached the building.

"Oh," Erin said as if now it all made sense, as if that were the reason behind everything tonight, the tears, the phone call. "Oh my God. When's the last time you even saw her?"

"At the trial," Paige said.

Erin pulled the car close enough to the curb so Paige could just reach out the window and drop it in. Paige's heart was racing. She felt another surge of emotions, sadness, anger, and something else. What was it? Why couldn't she identify it?

The letter was between her thumb and forefinger. She glanced at the address, scrawled in her eighth-grade handwriting: *David Bradley Lancaster, San Quentin State Prison.* She let it dangle there a few seconds before setting it free. It slipped down the chute without a sound.

"There," Paige said, rolling up her window. "There."

"Now what?" Erin said.

Now he would get the letter, probably thrilled to be hearing from someone from the outside world, and he would tear open the envelope, excited for what might be inside. Then he would read it and soon realize it was a reminder of that night—the night he ended a life and ruined twenty, fifty, one thousand others, including his own. It didn't matter if he read the whole thing, as long as he saw her signature at the bottom, *Paige Bellen,* because that way she'd get the final word.

"Home," Paige said. "I know I'm lame. It's Saturday night and I just want to go to bed." And while she was, indeed, exhausted, she thought she might have felt the slightest bit tingly, the way excitement makes you feel.

"It's okay," Erin said, pulling away from the curb. "I'm tired, too."

They drove back to the house, the baby and the ladybug. Erin parked in the driveway and let them in with her key. As soon as they entered the house, their mom called down from upstairs. "Is that you again, Erin?"

"It's both of us," Erin called back.

"Paige is home?" her mom said in an excited tone.

"Paige is home," Paige said.

"How was your party, honey?" her mom said.

"Fine," Paige said. "I'll tell you about it tomorrow."

Paige rolled her eyes as she and Erin climbed the stairs. Paige walked into her room and Erin followed.

"How was *your* party, by the way?" Paige asked unfastening the safety pins and letting her diaper/sheet fall to the floor. Halloween was over. She wasn't a baby anymore.

"Fun," Erin said, plopping herself on Paige's bed. "But I was the only dork dressed as a bug. Everyone else was all sexed up, well, the girls at least."

"I was the only baby, if it makes you feel better."

Paige peeled off her tights and put on the green flannel pajama bottoms Erin had given her last Christmas. She sat at her desk. She still had a letter to write to Caroline, so much to say now that the time had finally come where she might be able to move forward. She opened the middle drawer and for the first time in two years didn't see or feel the weight of that white envelope. On Monday it would be on its way. Perhaps on Tuesday it would arrive. Paige turned to Erin. "I'm sorry I got weird about your—"

"It's okay," Erin said. "You don't have to apologize."

"But you don't even know what I was about to say."

"My essay," Erin said. "I know."

"I don't *own* the story," Paige said.

For a second, Erin looked as though she might cry, but then it passed and her expression softened. "That was the worst night of my life," Erin said. "Because I thought something happened to you."

When Paige's parents had arrived frantic to Robin's house, Paige remembered wondering where Erin was. She worried she was home alone and what if the intruder came to their house next and took her? As it turned out, her parents had brought Erin to the neighbor's, and Paige was relieved.

"It did," Paige said. "Something did happen. It's still happening."

Erin sat up and took off her ladybug antennae. She scooted up the bed and rested her head on Paige's pillows. Paige joined her, leaning her head onto Erin's shoulder, like she did when they were little. "Snug as a bug in a rug," she said, echoing her parents' expression when they wrapped them in towels after bath time.

When Paige and her family finally returned home the night of the kidnapping it was around three thirty in the morning. There were several messages from Erin on the answering machine, the last being, "Come get me no matter what time you get home, please." Their dad went next door and returned a few minutes later with Erin in her blue bathrobe, who looked visibly shaken. Upstairs, Paige asked if she could sleep in Erin's bed and the girls squeezed in together under the covers, Paige still dizzy from fear, Erin unsure where to even begin. The next day, on the police's suggestion, they would move to a hotel for a few weeks, but for now, they were snug as bugs under the covers. Nothing had sunk in yet, nothing really made sense, but Paige's mind and body were so exhausted she managed to fall asleep, safe in the company of her big sister.

Paige now looked at the basket of stuffed animals next to her bed, Cinnamon's paw reaching out from it. How could she even fantasize about giving him away? He was Paige, really, in stuffed-animal form, once belonging to Robin and then suddenly one October night a witness, a bear witness. He was part of her personal narrative now, like a birthmark or a scar. Paige took a cue from him and reached her own arm around Erin.

"For good luck," she said, rubbing her hand up and down Erin's arm, because that's what ladybugs were supposed to bring.

Ninth Grade

"I'm okay," Paige said as they were leaving the house.

"I didn't say anything," her mom defended.

"You were giving me that look," Paige said.

"No look," her mom promised, her eyebrows furrowed and worried. "It's just my face."

It was the first day of the trial, almost two years since Robin was taken. Paige couldn't sleep the night before, her mind crowded and overflowing with memories and sadness. Caroline and her parents had flown in from Paris the night before and the families had met for dinner at San Pietro's because the girls wanted pizza, as if they could really eat anything. They hadn't seen each other in a year and a half, and Paige was struck by how sunny and fun Caroline still seemed to be. Paige spent the night trying to match Caroline's smile and keep up with her stories. Maybe taking her far away to another country is what Paige's parents should have done for her, too.

The trial had been delayed so many times that Paige put it out of her head. She had to. But when the date was finally set, Monday, September 13, her mind started spinning again as it had when she learned that Robin was dead. The prosecutors promised a swift resolution. The defense was pleading insanity, whatever that meant. Nevertheless, the trial was being held in Redwood City, over forty-five miles south of where the crime had occurred. Paige couldn't understand why everyone was concerned about a fair trial. Nothing about any of this was fair.

"Do you want to sit in front with Daddy?" her mom asked as they approached the car.

"No, thanks," Paige said, rolling her eyes so only her sister could see.

As the trial date neared, Paige went to see Dr. Swick twice a week. At her last session on Thursday he'd asked if she would feel more comfortable if he was there at the trial. At first she said, "No, no I'll be fine," but then very quickly changed her answer to "Yes." She thought seeing his calm, familiar face, or at least knowing he was in the room, might be just what she needed.

Paige coiled and then uncoiled a few strands of hair around her finger. Cinnamon, Robin's bear, was on her lap. When she buckled up, her instinct was to wrap him in the seat belt, too, but to protect him from what? He'd already experienced the loss of his owner. Caroline was bringing Rodney, Robin's other bear, which she'd dragged all the way from Paris. This would be a reunion for humans and bears alike.

Paige felt calm, detached even, until they began to cross the Golden Gate Bridge—a bridge she'd driven over hundreds, if not thousands, of times—a bridge she normally loved, but now, suddenly, things didn't feel normal. She was gripped with a fear that the bridge would unhinge and collapse, tossing everybody into the water with it. They were stuck in traffic and Paige told herself not to look out the window, not to look down, but she couldn't help it and did anyway. She tapped her foot to the beat of her quickening heart.

"You're kicking my seat," her mom said, but Paige didn't stop. She wrapped her arms snug around Cinnamon. Out of the corner of her eye she could see Erin watching her.

There were television vans, camera crews, and reporters outside of the courthouse. Paige worried that she'd be caught in the mayhem again, microphones thrust in her face, journalists asking questions she couldn't begin to answer, but her father had been given instructions to bring the car around to the back of the building where they would be met by a liaison who would take them into a private holding room. As they made a right onto the side street, she could see the chaotic media scene—hordes of people, lights, cameras, and microphones. Paige didn't know how it would work from there, except that there would be a moment when David Bradley Lancaster would enter. Dr. Swick said she didn't have to look at him and that once he sat down his back would be toward her so he wouldn't be able to see her either; at least not until later, when she was called to the stand as a witness.

Paige wondered, as they passed through the security check inside the building, what she would have been doing on this day, Monday, September 13 had it been just a regular day. Her alternate life, the one also killed by David Bradley Lancaster, came into her imagination every now and then, but it remained mostly blurry and just out of reach.

"You must be so relieved this day is finally here," the court liaison said once they were seated in the holding room. She was wearing a badge that signified importance. It was tied to a yellow ribbon around her neck.

Everyone looked at Paige as she numbly answered, "Yeah."

There was a platter of vegetables and a pitcher of water on the table. The liaison took a carrot before exiting the room.

Paige's mom sighed.

Erin chewed at a cuticle.

Her dad was lost in thought.

The liaison returned with Robin's dad, and Paige's mom unsuccessfully choked back tears as she stood to hug him. Mr. Hecht looked angry. His eyes narrowed and his mouth was in a perpetual scowl. But the thing was, he always looked that way, even before Robin was taken. It seemed only now that his expression matched the mood. When he saw Paige, he put an arm around her and squeezed her close, without saying a word. Soon the room was filled with Caroline and her parents and Robin's mom and her dad, Robin's grandfather. The last time Paige had seen this configuration of people was within the hour that Robin was taken, as everyone moved around dazed in their living room two years ago.

"You girls are so big," Robin's mom said.

Paige willed herself to be smaller.

Two of the lawyers came in next—a short man with glasses and a woman in a fashionable skirted suit. The woman approached Paige and smiled warmly. "Finally," she said with conviction. "I know there is nothing pleasant about this for you," she added, "but at this point the law is the only resolution we have." Paige wasn't sure how to respond, but she didn't have to because Caroline joined them.

"I want to be a criminal prosecutor when I'm older," she told the lawyer.

How was it that Caroline could see her future so clearly when Paige could barely put one foot in front of the other?

"You'll make an excellent attorney," the lawyer said to Caroline. "I just know it."

The room was starting to feel hot from all of the people in it. Someone else entered and introduced herself as the victims' rights advocate. There were so many people to keep track of, so many official badges dangling around people's necks. Caroline took Paige's hand and led her over to the vegetable platter. "I'm worried about you," she whispered. "You're being so quiet."

"I'm fine," Paige said too quickly.

"You're not fine. No one here is fine."

"I know."

"You're allowed to be mad," Caroline said. "You're allowed to be sad."

Caroline was starting to sound like Dr. Swick.

"Just so you know, I'm planning on burning a hole through him with my stare," Caroline said, taking her friend's hand.

Paige didn't have the guts to confess that she didn't think she'd even be able to look at him.

When it was time, the liaison led them into the actual courtroom, which was familiar to her from the law shows she watched on television, but much smaller than Paige had anticipated. Her heart raced. A small railing separated the spectators from the principal players. Both sections were teeming with people. Filing down the center aisle, Paige was surprised by all of the familiar faces—so many of her classmates, and here she thought everyone else was having a regular day at school. The parade stalled as people spread into their seats, and Paige found herself standing next to Kaj who was sitting on the aisle. She was surprised when he took her dangling hand and gave it a squeeze. It was the first time she felt his touch since last year in her room on her bed.

Caroline and Paige sat next to each other on the stiff, wooden benches, bears on laps. People kept leaning up and over to acknowledge them with touches and winks. Paige wondered who the cluster of people was to the right until she realized it was the jury—twelve of them sitting on benches, too. The press, twenty or so people on the opposite end of the room, were already scribbling on pads of paper and typing on laptops, even though nothing had yet begun. Peripherally, Paige could sense one of the jurors gazing at her and she didn't like the feeling of being seen.

There was an audible hum in the room. The press was fidgeting with gadgets and people were speaking above a whisper. Paige was nervous about what was coming next. Once the judge appeared, the criminal would appear. It was all because of him that they were here, at this formal gathering of the very worst kind.

In the row ahead and to the left of Paige, an artist was sketching the scene in front of him. She liked the way his hand moved the charcoal across the page. Watching him caused a sort of hypnotic sensation, so much so that she didn't take notice of the hush that enveloped the room. When she gazed up, cross-checking the accuracy of the court reporter to the drawing, she saw David Bradley Lancaster, in handcuffs and an orange jumpsuit, being ushered across the room to the defense table. She hadn't seen him since identifying him in the lineup almost two years ago and in that time he'd deflated—that was the only way to describe it. He looked like a giant balloon once and now it was like the air had been leeched from him. His hair was long and wild, and he seemed annoyed at being there. The guard hovered over him as he took a seat next to his lawyers. Paige could see profiles of the defense team. They were busy shuffling through papers. No one really looked at him. Paige caught a glimpse of the artist's rendering of David Bradley Lancaster but turned away so she wouldn't have to see the details.

Caroline was openly crying and her sister, Erin, was wiping away tears, too. Paige didn't understand why she couldn't feel anything—not sadness, not hatred, not fear.

"Are you okay?" her mom mouthed.

Paige barely nodded yes.

Someone stood and began to speak. "All rise for the honorable Judge Beyman." And now there was no turning back. Paige stood with everyone else. She was in the third row, closer to the jury box, far from the defense table, but not far enough away.

The judge entered, robed and looking like Alfred Hitchcock. He took his seat on the bench and banged the gavel. Everyone sat back down. "Good morning," he said, organizing some papers in front of him. "We're here in the matter of the United States of America versus David Bradley Lancaster." Paige liked how that sounded. With all of America against him, there was no way he could be set free.

The prosecution team assembled a photo stand and placed on it a giant picture of Robin, not the one that had been used on all the *Missing* fliers pasted across town, but a casual picture of her and Briscoe, Robin smiling and hugging her dog. The photograph was taken by her father the day he took the girls to the beach, not long before the crime, where they splayed out on the sand and formed letters for an alphabet book her dad never completed. Paige had a moment to gaze at the picture, adorable Robin staring back at her, before the lawyer angled it toward the jury. Within moments the lawyer with the glasses was standing in front of the jury. His opening statement would mark a new chapter in this horror story.

"Are you okay?" her sister asked as they were walking back to the car.

"Yes," Paige snapped.

Up ahead, she saw her parents look at each other.

Earlier in the month there was talk about getting a hotel room for the duration of the trial, but they decided that Redwood City was too far from day-to-day life. Paige's dad took a week off from work, and if it seemed like the trial would drag on past that, he'd take more time.

They piled into the car and headed home.

"I think we should get a hotel room," Paige said loudly from the backseat as they were stuck in traffic on the 101 Freeway.

"I think she's right," her mom said quickly. "I'm not going to be able to do this commute every day."

Court had let out at three o'clock. It was now four thirty and they'd only just crossed the dreaded bridge.

"I'll make a reservation for tomorrow until Friday," her dad said, relenting.

"Can we stay at Caroline's hotel?" Paige asked.

"They're at the Stanford Park," her mom said.

"No," her dad said. "We're not staying there. I'll call the Best Western."

They finally made their way through town and deposited the car back in their garage. Paige walked straight upstairs and into her bed, where she burrowed under the covers and forced herself to sleep.

Before Robin was taken, Paige thought death was something that came slowly, with warning, the way that cancer had taken her grandfather—her father's father—when she was ten. There were phone calls and hospital visits that continued over a period of a year. As he got sicker, he got grayer, hairier, and skinnier until he finally disappeared. There was talk about how young he was, but Paige didn't understand. He was sixty-six and that seemed really old to her, seemed about the right age for someone to die. It was Robin who had comforted her the next day at school when Paige felt teary at lunch. Robin followed her to the bathroom to make sure she was okay. Robin's empathy had felt special to Paige. Two years later when Paige heard Robin was gone, when her parents sat her down in the living room to confront the horrible news, Paige pictured her grandfather toward the end of his life, on the hospital bed, and replaced his image with an image of Robin, tubes in her nose, an IV in her arm. Though cancer was not the cause of Robin's death, it was the only way Paige could take in the information, could visualize Robin's transition from life to death.

The next day, after another long commute into Redwood City, Mom and Dad in the front seat, Paige, Erin, and Cinnamon in back, they met again in the holding room. Everyone but Robin was there. Earlier in the process, the prosecution had told them that they were planning on telling the story backwards, starting with the police who had discovered Robin's body and ending with the night she was taken, the night she spent with Caroline and Paige. After, they would show pictures and videos of Robin. They said they felt the case would be stronger, would resonate more with the jurors, if they were left with the image of Robin alive and loving life. Today's witnesses would be members of the police department, perhaps some that Paige had already met.

When they marched into the courtroom, Paige noticed there were just as many people, but the faces had changed. Yesterday her science teacher, Mr. Kholos, had been there, but today she didn't see him, instead Madame Boyle, her French teacher, was in attendance. Paige nodded when she saw Dr. Swick in the fourth row, next to Kaj again, who nodded back. The artist was still sketching, the press still scribbling. Paige and her family made their way to the third row, where they'd been seated yesterday, as reporters took the stand, reiterating the story from their point of view.

After court, Paige and her family checked into the Comfort Inn, because the Best Western was booked. The hotel was as plain and boring and beige as the one they'd checked into after Robin's disappearance two years ago. Once they were settled in their rooms, her dad grabbed the car keys and drove Paige the four miles to Palo Alto, where Caroline was staying.

In the car they were quiet first, but as they approached the hotel, with its sprawling front garden, her dad looked at Paige solemnly. "Paigey," he said, sighing, "what I wouldn't give for you to never have experienced this." She then thought she saw tears forming in his eyes and she couldn't bear the sight of his crying so she looked out her window.

She stupidly said, "It's okay." But of course they both knew it wasn't.

Caroline was waiting in the hotel lobby when she arrived, already wearing a bathing suit and carrying a towel. Paige had brought hers along in a backpack, but she didn't much feel like swimming.

"Are you okay?" Those were the first words out of Caroline's mouth.

"Yeah," Paige said. What did she look like that everyone always asked her that? Of course Paige wasn't okay. This time she was drowning in the image of her father and the pained expression on his face as he drove away.

"Don't you wanna go swimming?" Caroline asked, gently. "You're not wearing your suit."

"I have it," Paige said pointing to her backpack. "But maybe I'll just lie on a chair and watch you swim."

"Really?" Caroline said. "That's no fun. For you."

Paige shrugged.

They headed outside. The hotel had beautiful grounds, a pool, a Jacuzzi, and an outside bar. Caroline stepped out of her shorts and T-shirt. She was wearing a blue, checkered bikini with ruffles on the bottom. She was very tall, at least four inches taller than Paige, and willowy. "You are so lucky," she called out to Paige who was settling in on a lounge chair. "Do you even know how cold it is in Paris right now? Like five degrees Celsius," Caroline said.

"I don't know what that means," Paige confessed.

"Oh," Caroline said, stepping into the pool, "that's like, forty-one degrees Fahrenheit."

Paige watched Caroline splash around, and then start to do laps. After about half an hour she joined Paige on the empty lounge chair next to her, toweling off. "I needed that," Caroline said, tilting her face toward the sun. "What have you been doing to get rid of stress?" she asked.

"I was playing a lot of volleyball," Paige said.

"Oh, I bet that's great, punching the ball and everything," Caroline said. "And running around whacking it over the net. I can totally see you doing that."

"Yeah," Paige said. Should she tell her that she quit the team last year for no good reason?

"What else do you do?"

"For stress? I've been in therapy since seventh grade," she said.

"No, I mean physically. Volleyball and . . . do you go biking or running or hiking?"

"No."

"Who do you hang out with?"

"I don't know," Paige said.

"How do you not know who you hang out with?" Caroline said.

"I don't really 'hang out,'" Paige said. Sure, she hung out in front of the TV and in her bedroom. Once she hung out in her bedroom with Kaj, but she didn't think that was Caroline's business.

"Do you have a boyfriend?" Caroline prodded.

That wasn't fair. Caroline knew she didn't. Why would she ask if she already knew the answer? Paige shook her head no.

"I don't know if I *technically* have a boyfriend," Caroline said, "but I've been spending a lot of time with JC. This guy Jean-Christophe. He's a year older than me and totally gorgeous."

"Wow," Paige said.

"He's, like, one of the only people who knows about this. You're so lucky you don't have to explain it to anyone. You don't even know how weird it is."

This was the third time Caroline called Paige "lucky" and maybe Paige had it all wrong, but she didn't feel lucky at all.

People called her that after the incident as well. "Lucky to be alive" was a phrase she heard over and over. Her good luck was Robin's bad luck. That's how she saw it.

"Actually, *you* seem like the lucky one, Caroline," Paige said, sitting up. "You have a boyfriend, you live in Paris, you do things to get rid of your stress."

"You sound mad," Caroline said too quickly. "Don't be mad, I'm just trying to be a friend. I'm just . . . we're worried about you."

"Who's 'we'?" Paige said, suddenly feeling on the verge of tears herself.

"Me, my mom, your mom, your sister. . . ."

"When did you talk to my sister?"

"At the courthouse and at dinner the other night."

Paige had no recollection of any significant interaction between the two of them.

"I know you're in therapy but do you think it's working?" Caroline said.

Her words stung, because she knew that Caroline's family didn't believe in therapy. She had only gone to a few sessions herself before her parents pulled her out.

Paige's dad had dropped her off only half an hour ago but she was ready to be picked up. She didn't want to have dinner with Caroline's family anymore. She didn't want to be in this fancy, fake hotel.

"You're my best friend," Caroline was saying. "I don't have sisters; you're my sister."

No, she was Erin's sister, and Erin's sister only.

"I miss my old Paigey," Caroline said taking Paige's hand and shaking it, like she was trying to shake the life back into her. Paige squirmed out of her grasp.

"I'm not like you," Paige said.

"You have this look in your eyes like you're about to say something, but you never say it. It's like no one knows what you're thinking. You need to have it out, Paige. You need to punch something."

At this moment it was Caroline that Paige wanted to punch.

"JC's been such a—"

"I should go," Paige said, standing up.

Caroline jumped up, too. "No!" she said. "You can't leave, you just got here!"

"I'm obviously not good company," Paige said, collecting her backpack from the ground.

"You are so good company!" Caroline begged. "You're the only person on the planet who I can be myself with! Paige, we're together for life. We're like conjoined twins."

"Conjoined twins separated by the Atlantic Ocean?"

"Yeah," Caroline laughed. "The Atlantic is running between our two fat heads!"

Paige sat back down but Caroline stayed standing. "I think this trial is actually gonna be good for you," she said in her knowing tone. "This could be, like, the final thing you need before you move on."

Paige wanted so badly to believe her. What if, once the trial was done, assuming he was found guilty, she was able to store the experience, the memory away, like her old stuffed animals in the basket under her bed? She barely remembered those animals were even there anymore. "Maybe," Paige said.

"I miss you so much," Caroline said, and bent down to hug her, staining Paige's dry clothes with pool water. "*Ma soeur, ma meilleure amie.*"

"We call to the witness stand Paige Renee Bellen," a female voice said. This was it. Paige took a deep breath. The judge spoke. "Paige Bellen, please come forward and be sworn in. Ms. Bellen, right up here in front of the clerk of the court." It was now her turn, finally. The police had spoken, the detectives, the reporters, the head of the search team, a prison guard, and some neighbors also had their turn on the stand. All this talking had taken up two weeks and now finally on a Friday at eleven thirty, Paige was called to tell her story.

She stood and made her way to the gate that separated the judge from the spectators. Everything played out in slow motion. As she exited her row, her mom reached out for her, as did her sister. What were they doing? It was so embarrassing. Someone lead her through the gate and she began to take her stance in order to be sworn in. "Ms. Bellen," the judge said in his booming voice, "we only need you as the witness, not the bear," and that's when she realized she was still holding Cinnamon. That's what her mom and sister had been reaching for, the bear. She thought she heard people laughing. She was embarrassed she was carrying a teddy bear and wasn't sure what to do with it now that it had accompanied her to the witness stand. Should she toss it back over to her mom? Give it to the prosecution team? Someone approached her, a guard, and took Cinnamon from her. "Thank you," the judge said to the guard. "And don't forget to return it," he said, perhaps jokingly, wagging his finger. Paige watched the guard walk off with the bear thinking to herself how silly he looked, and as she turned back to the judge, she mistakenly met the eyes of David Bradley Lancaster, sitting to her left, also watching the scene play out. It was fleeting, their joined gaze, but in that second she experienced the darkness, his shadow, almost like a dimming of the soul—his coal eyes dead behind their lids. The connection flustered her at first, and then it sickened her. The truth was that there was no avoiding him. She was gripped by an odd and loud grumble of her stomach, a pinching, a cramp, and then a rank taste in her mouth, dry and metallic. It passed as quickly as it came on, because seeing him fueled her, too.

"Please raise your right hand," the clerk said.

She did.

"Paige Renee Bellen, called as a witness at the request of the plaintiff, having been first duly sworn on oath, is examined and testifies as follows," the clerk announced.

Paige said, "Yes."

"Thank you. Please take your seat."

Paige sat on the edge of her seat, a new resolve taking over her. She was the voice that he couldn't silence. Oh, he had tried to stuff her face into a pillow but she found her way out of that, too.

"Please state your name for the record?" the prosecutor said.

"Paige Renee Bellen."

Someone else approached the stand and adjusted the microphone in front of Paige. She eyed the glass of water next to her. Her mouth was already so dry. She didn't know how she was going to get through this.

"Why don't you try that again," the judge said.

"Paige Renee Bellen," she said again, and this time she heard her forceful voice amplified throughout the little courtroom. She felt it bounce across the wooden walls and land plunk! in front of the criminal himself. She caught a glimpse of Caroline in the front row, nodding her on in encouragement. All that was left of Robin was her name, but Paige had both her name and her story. Paige still had her voice; he couldn't ever kill that.

Once upon a time three best friends were playing and then the Big Bad Wolf huffed and he puffed and he blew the house down.

She cleared her throat in anticipation of what was to come, of what she hoped would finally be the beginning of the end of the story.

Eighth Grade

Paige woke to find Erin puking in a trash can. "Oh my God," Paige said from the inflatable mattress on the floor, "Are you okay?"

"No," Erin winced. "Go get Mom."

Paige flung the covers off and ran into her parents' room down the hall. "Mom," she said, quick and breathy, "Erin needs you."

Both her parents flew out of bed, like a choreographed dance, and raced down the hall. Paige wondered if their sleep was as restless as her own ever since the incident, if they woke to every creak of the house, every bump in the night as she did.

"I don't feel right," Erin said, bits of gunk now in her hair, on her bed, on the floor. The room was starting to smell.

"You're burning," her mom said, her hand first on Erin's forehead, then her cheek and neck. "Get a thermometer. Someone."

Paige ran into their shared bathroom to find one. The family waited around the bed and when her temperature was announced (102.2°F), their dad escorted Paige out of the room.

"What's wrong with her?" Paige said, worried.

"Probably the flu," her dad said. "That's my guess." Paige followed him into his room. "Do you think you can try to sleep in your own room?" he asked, cautiously. "Just for tonight?"

Paige hadn't slept in her own bed since the night before Robin was taken, almost a year ago now. The hotel they'd temporarily moved into after the crime was a sterile, beige hotel, and for those two weeks she shared a queen-size bed with Erin. Upon returning home, her parents, with Erin's approval, plugged in the blow-up mattress they used for guests and that's where Paige stayed for the next ten months.

It wasn't as if Paige disliked her room, her bed, the comfort of her own space, it was that Paige just couldn't muster up the courage to be alone anymore, either while awake or asleep.

She could hear the sound of sheets being changed in the other room, the *whoosh* of the clean sheet as her mom released it from its folds, and then the sound of Erin throwing up again, this time in the bathroom. "Eeew," Paige said, covering her ears and stomping her feet like a football player.

Her dad started heading in the direction of Paige's room. "You think you can try your room?" he said again.

"I don't know," Paige said. "I guess."

"Just try, kiddo," he said, giving her an encouraging look. "It's three in the morning. You need to get back to sleep."

Her mom was still fussing in the other room. Paige said good night to her dad and followed the hallway down to her own room.

"I love you," her dad called.

"Love you," she answered.

Moonlight came through the window, providing natural light for Paige. It's not as though she hadn't spent any time in her room. She did homework there, talked on the phone, changed outfits, wrote in her diary, and even took a few naps on her bed, though never under the covers. She knew she couldn't spend the rest of her life in Erin's room, on Erin's floor, but she always thought she'd sense when the time was right to move back. Perhaps Mother Nature sensed it for her. It would be good to get back to her bed, she thought. It would be right.

She walked in cautious but prepared. She threw the two big, yellow decorative pillows off the bed and pulled back the covers with one big swoop. In the next room her mom was murmuring something and Erin was groaning in response. It was helpful hearing their voices, even though she couldn't make out the specifics. Once settled, Paige looked around.

The night cast shadows on her walls, but that's all they were—refractions of light. The front door was locked, she knew because she checked it every night. Windows were sealed. The street outside was silent. She looked at the clock next to her bed. It read 3:25.

In the time after she was taken and before she was found, Robin's image was everywhere—wrapped around neighborhood telephone poles, plastered on walls in the post office, creased and folded into the newspaper, and on all sorts of programs on television. Talk radio even devoted time to the story. Each day that Robin wasn't found, Paige experienced mounting anxiety. When she expressed this to Dr. Swick, he suggested she turn off the television, turn off the radio, and instead listen to classical music on her CD or record player. Her mom dug through her own music collection and extracted a dozen classical albums and CDs, and Paige found comfort in going to bed listening to Chopin's études and nocturnes, and Bach's keyboard suites. She wondered how many other twelve-year-olds found pleasure and relief in that music. It was a necessity for Paige, a break from a news story that might have caught her off guard.

Paige tuned the clock radio to the classical station, 91.5, and tried to settle down listening to Pachelbel's Canon.

"You're okay?" her mom said, whispering, yet knocking Paige out of her reverie.

"I guess?" Paige said.

Somehow, she fell asleep, and in the morning she thought, perhaps, that she was one step closer to normalcy.

It was odd that Paige found such success with volleyball when it was Erin who was the family athlete. Paige felt she was always playing catch-up with Erin, and when she did finally catch up, it was only momentarily until Erin jumped ahead again, like an endless game of leapfrog.

Paige found volleyball when Erin was in tenth grade at another school, the high school, excelling in soccer and every other sport she liked to play. Paige's wrists and arms were blue and purple from bruises but the pain felt right, and to see actual proof of the pain? Even better. Volleyball was good for Paige because every serve was bashing his head. Every dunk was drowning him. She ran for each ball with speed and determination. Everyone knew she was the closer. There were girls who were good at the setup, but Paige always delivered the final slam. Although she was just in eighth grade, her coach was already praising her athleticism, suggesting the scholarships for which she'd be qualified for college. College! Such an incredible idea! She was still trying to get through the days of junior high, she could barely imagine a future five years down the road.

Volleyball filled the physical and mental void—when her mind started spiraling and skipping backwards, started filling her head with images of that night last year in October, or even worse, of Robin's body in a shallow ditch. She would whack a ball and it would snap her out of her daymare. Volleyball was good for her, good for the team, for the school. Her friends rallied around her at games screaming from the bleachers, "Go, Paige!" She loved the squeak of her shoes on the gym floor, like little birds chirping. She loved being part of a team, loved moving with them as a unit.

In volleyball, Paige wasn't alone; she didn't stand out. On her own, she'd have to field sad glances, endure whispers and points. She imagined what they were saying: *That's the one! The girl who was there when Robin was taken,* or worse, *the girl who let Robin get taken.* She could hide in a team. In pictures for the yearbook, she could just be the brown-haired girl in the back row.

In November, Paige went to her first bat mitzvah. She'd been friends with Debbie Schneider since the third grade. Her dad dropped her off at the synagogue where she met up with Sofia and Beth, dressed formally for the occasion. Her friends were still her friends but a strange and unspoken distance had now emerged between them. It was as though they'd all taken a giant step back, like a permanent hokeypokey.

"I like your skirt," Paige said to Beth as they entered the temple.

"I like your shoes," Sofia told Paige.

This is what they said. It was socially acceptable. Much better than "Robin can't be here because she was murdered," which is what was looping through Paige's mind.

The service was hard to sit through, as everything—class, lunch, dinner, you name it—had been for her lately. Throughout the ceremony, her girlfriends escaped to the bathroom two by two, and the guys fidgeted and poked at each other. Paige wanted to pay attention, she did, but her mind drifted out and above Debbie who was singing something in Hebrew.

Sometimes, when she simply didn't have the energy to stop herself from thinking, didn't have it in her to snap the rubber band or yell, "Stop!" as Dr. Swick had suggested, Paige found herself, as she did now, in temple, picturing what happened to Robin after the intruder carried her out of the house, slung over his shoulders like a sack of rice.

"Please put me down," she imagined Robin saying weakly, probably too shocked for tears. He would have assured her, as he did them, that nothing would happen if she just kept quiet, and knowing Robin, she probably did just that.

He put her in the car—the front seat? The back? The trunk? Paige assumed the trunk because wouldn't Robin have flung open the door and run as fast as she could to get out?

Paige wondered what route they took once they pulled away from Golden Lane. Did they go left on Laurel, right on Cyprus, and another right on Spring Street, winding through the center of town, passing the post office, the bakery, the antique stores, her mom's tea shop, and eventually Miller Middle School on the way to the freeway? Or had they departed the back way, a left on Laurel, a left on Oak, and then a right on Church, past a few empty lots, a power plant, church, lumberyard, and then the old, dark highway. What had Robin been thinking? Or was she somehow able to let her mind go blank, black as the night, with no fear, no sadness, no worry.

In the beginning, Paige never doubted that Robin would return home, not once. In the first hour of her disappearance Paige could only process it as a gross mistake. This sort of thing didn't happen to people she knew. The intruder got the house wrong. It should have been happening next door, or a few houses down. Within the second hour of her disappearance, Paige gave the intruder the benefit of the doubt, assuming he'd recognize the error of his ways, feel bad that he snatched an innocent girl from her bedroom, and would return her, tail between his legs, with an apology. By the third hour, she came to believe that the police would catch him, and Robin would return in a car with sirens blaring, a dramatic homecoming, but a homecoming nonetheless. Robin would describe the scene in great detail, and they'd continue where they left off, Paige and Robin jumping on the bed.

That night, when Paige's parents arrived (Paige still wasn't even sure how they knew—had Robin's mom called them? Or was it that tall, cute police guy?) Paige took in a little more of the horror. The expression on her dad's gentle face was so mangled and desperate. Her parents circled her, clutching her and crying. Only later did Paige notice her mom's outfit—a nightgown and jeans, and a blue raincoat, even though it was balmy and dry.

Members of the FBI had arrived and a flurry of activity ensued. They fanned out, dusting for prints in Robin's room, interviewing a tearful Mrs. Hecht in the kitchen and Caroline in the living room. At some point, Mr. Hecht arrived at the house, bewildered and stormy. Their divorce had been finalized six months earlier, but now this crisis was already bringing them back together. Paige couldn't wait to tell Robin about the scene unfolding in her house. It was all so surreal.

And where was Robin exactly during all of this? If he'd taken the back way, to the old highway as Paige had imagined, they'd be driving in the dark. Later, she'd learn about the piece of news that made everyone cringe and cry, the grim reality of human carelessness. They learned police, who hadn't yet heard of the abduction, had pulled the intruder's car over for speeding. Oh, where was Robin when the sirens sounded and the car stopped, two officers approaching and asking the intruder to step outside. If she was in the trunk, why didn't she kick and scream? Was it possible she didn't know it was the police? Was she paralyzed with fear? Was she even still alive?

When Paige's mind returned to the present, the rabbi was parading around the room with the giant Torah, people kissing their fingers and pressing them firmly against the scrolls. Debbie was behind him and behind her were her grandparents, three of them, and a couple of young boys, her brothers. It was like a conga line, only somber and important.

Paige wondered if Debbie truly believed in God, or was this merely part of the rite of passage. And if she did, how could she account for the crime against Robin? In what way could this religion help explain her murder?

Paige scanned the room. Beth and Sofia were returning from the bathroom. Kaj was fingering his yarmulke. Bruce's leg was shaking in boredom. Were any of her friends thinking about murder and God as well?

The bat mitzvah party was in a large banquet room of a nearby hotel. The kids stayed near the DJ and dance floor while the adults milled around the bar at the opposite end. This was Paige's first bat mitzvah, though she already had invitations to two others in the coming months. She wondered if they would all be alike.

The DJ started off with the cha-cha slide, the dance they did at all parties and school dances. Paige jumped into formation next to Beth and Sofia as they followed instructions: *to the left, one hop back, to the right, one check.* She looked around at everyone having a great time—Bruce hamming it up, Debbie flailing her arms, even some grown-ups were following along. But Paige felt like she was outside of herself, watching a hollowed out doll go through the motions. Sure, she was smiling and singing along, but where was the fun? Why did she always feel like she was missing out? She joined the line for the buffet, chatted with friends, posed for silly pictures in the photo booth, built an ice-cream sundae, all without feeling.

As late afternoon slipped into early evening, there came a part of the party when Debbie called on certain family members to join her in lighting candles in her honor. Paige watched halfheartedly as Debbie's brothers came up; her grandparents and some cousins followed. "There are people who couldn't be here today," she said, her voice quivering in the microphone. "There are people that I'd like to honor. In Robin Hecht's memory, I'd like to call my friend Paige Bellen up to light a candle."

Paige heard the words but she wasn't connecting to them. She looked around and saw the grown-ups gazing at her and she thought she sensed a hush in the room.

"Are you okay?" Beth whispered to her, and when she looked at Beth she saw tears, and then realized people were applauding, some even whistling. What was it for? Debbie? The event? Robin? Beth nudged her a little and Paige stepped forward, crossing the dance floor toward where Debbie was standing, holding out an unlit candle.

Debbie looked so pretty in her blue dress. Was it the same dress she'd worn during the service a few hours ago? How had Paige not noticed before? The blue brought out her eyes, or maybe it was the mascara she was wearing. "I love you," Debbie said, handing Paige the candle.

Shit, Paige thought, why hadn't she paid attention to the others who went before her? She didn't know what to do with that candle, which suddenly reminded her of the vigil that was held in Johnson Square before Robin had been found, when there was still hope, so much that it lit the town in a warm glow. Paige took the candle and glanced at the others that had already been lit. "Ummm," she muttered, and Debbie took her hand and brought it down to the light where it caught the flame and danced bright.

"Robin should have been here today," Debbie whispered, as Paige set the candle down with the others. "But thank God you're here." Debbie wrapped her small arms around Paige, who felt tears on her bare shoulders. Paige held her, but couldn't muster tears herself. Her mind was simply too crowded with images to make way for emotions.

Somehow, she found her way back to her friends, some of whom were sobbing in the corner; others were more composed. Worried about Paige, they offered her water and hugs. Paige thought about the next bat mitzvahs, the ones in late November and early December and decided right there that she wouldn't attend. She didn't want to be the one who brought the whole party to tears.

Paging Paige,
        Sometimes I get this weird feeling that everything before now was a dream, or a nightmare, depending on how you look at it, and this has been my only reality. Other times being here in Paris feels like the dream and everything before was harsh reality. The kids at school seem nice enough, though it's still

so early in the year that it's hard to know for sure. I haven't really told any of them about what happened at home, only that my dad got transferred for work, which, of course, is only half the story. What's the point of moving to France if you can't at least get a fresh start, right? Don't worry, I'll be back next year. Until then, you have to give me all the gossip in your next letter. Whose class are you in? How's Beth? Sofia? Gus? Kaj? When is Debbie's bat mitzvah? Kenny's at college in New York. The water bed is still in his room at home. I wonder if the renters are using it? By the way, have you met the renters yet? Their daughter is our age and going to Miller, too. Jonathan and Randy are sharing a room, but I have my own on the third floor of our house. At first my parents thought I'd be happier in the room next to them, but I love it up here. It feels really safe to be so high and so far away. One thing I've been dying to tell you is that I got pizza sauce. Did you? You have to promise to let me know. Sometimes I dream about me, you, and Robin just hanging out and I wake up in the best mood, and then slowly I remember. It's such a shock every, single time. I miss you sooooo much. Come visit!

Avec amour,
Sweet Caroline

Three months after sailing along as the volleyball team champ, Paige awoke one day feeling deflated. She had practice later that afternoon and then a game the next day after school, but suddenly she couldn't picture herself being able to serve. In the past, she'd simply throw the ball up and pound it over the net, but now when she thought about it, she wondered how the ball had enough energy to actually make it over? In her mind, the air had leaked out of her like a flat volleyball.

"I think I'm going to quit volleyball," she told Dr. Swick at her therapy appointment later that day.

"Really?" he said, adjusting the thermostat. "I thought it was something that brought you a lot of joy—a positive thing for you to focus on."

Paige shook her head no. "Not anymore. It's getting in the way."

"Of school?"

"Of everything," she lied.

"Can you be more specific?"

Paige shrugged. "No."

"I've only ever heard you speak enthusiastically about volleyball," he said, "so I'm wondering if something happened to change your mind."

She felt like a loser because nothing had happened, nothing new on top of last year's tragedy. It was like a light switch had just suddenly flicked off.

"I'd like to encourage you to give it another go," he said. "Why don't you see how you feel tomorrow before you make any rash decisions?"

And the next day, after a lackluster practice, Paige approached the coach and told her that she was truly sorry, but she wasn't going to play for the team anymore.

"Volleyball isn't solely about volleyball," Coach Hopkins said. "It's about life skills, too, and about the support of a team and daily measurements of confidence."

Paige shook her head no.

"What can I do to make you stay?" the coach pleaded.

"I'm sorry," Paige said again, "nothing."

After her last practice, where her teammates glumly hugged and high fived her, expressing how much they'd miss her, she waited on the steps outside of school for her mom to pick her up. Kaj was on the steps, too, waiting for his dad to pick him up from tennis. Paige couldn't remember where he was from originally—the Philippines? The Bahamas? Geography was not her strong suit, but Kaj had sweet, sad eyes and sun-kissed skin. He'd always been a scrappy kid, but during the summer of seventh grade he had a growth spurt and when he arrived back to school, he'd blossomed. They'd always made small talk, waiting for their parents to pick them up. This time she confessed to him that she had quit the team.

"Really?" he said.

"Don't you ever get tired of tennis?" she asked.

"I love it," Kaj said. "When the season's over, I play at the park."

Paige didn't feel the same way about volleyball, and it only confirmed that she had made the right decision.

"So this is the end of our stoop chats?" he said.

"I guess so," Paige said. "Do you ever want to maybe come over and do homework or something?" She wasn't sure why she'd just invited him over. Perhaps it was another connection to Robin she didn't want to break.

Kaj shrugged. "Okay," he said.

She would have a lot more free time now that she'd ditched volleyball. Her dad stayed in San Francisco late on Tuesdays and Erin had soccer practice until six, the same time her mom closed the shop. "How about next Tuesday?" she suggested.

"Sounds good," Kaj said. "I can walk to your house from here, right?" he asked.

Sure he could. Anyone could, anyone but Paige. Her parents kept a tight leash on her now, a regular ole choke chain.

"Right," she said, as her mom pulled up to the curb.

Inside the car, her mom looked hopeful until Paige confirmed she had quit the team. "Look on the bright side. Now you don't have to pick me up anymore," Paige said, forcing a smile. Her mom did not look pleased.

The next Tuesday, before Kaj arrived, Paige nudged the basket of stuffed animals under her bed; she didn't want to look like a little girl. When he arrived she brought him upstairs and he sat on the bay window ledge while Paige sat on her bed. It was strange seeing a guy in her room. She gazed around her space through his point of view, seeing the yellow daisy wallpaper, her bookshelves, her bed all in a new light. She'd been in the same room since she was an infant, now instead of a crib she had a bed, instead of a changing table, bookshelves.

"Cool view," Kaj said. Her window faced the street and looked out over the neighbor's house. There was nothing really cool about it.

"My sister has the cool view," she said. "She faces the backyard."

"You get to watch over the street," Kaj said, hopping off the window ledge and joining her on the bed. "You could be, like, the mayor of Loring Road."

Paige smiled.

Out of nowhere, Kaj asked, "Do you ever think about that night?"

Paige knew what he meant and her breathing immediately intensified.

"I'm sorry," Kaj said. "I didn't mean to—"

"No, it's okay," she said in a soft voice, "I think about it every day."

"I do, too," Kaj said. "And I wasn't even there."

"I know," Paige said. What she meant was she knew he thought about it. Everyone at school, even teachers and the principal, must have thought about it every day. Miller Middle School was now forever linked to Robin's story.

"Sometimes," Kaj said, "I trick myself into believing she just transferred to Allenton or something."

"I know," Paige said again. "So do I." All the excitement of Kaj—having him in her room, on her bed—was starting to slip away. She wondered if he'd forged a friendship with her all for Robin, all because of Robin.

"What was it like?" he asked, looking down at his feet. "I mean, you don't have to talk about it if you don't want. . . ."

The crime wasn't taboo conversation, it couldn't be. In the weeks before Robin was found, most of the community came out for support, hanging signs, manning phones, spreading out on foot to search. Kaj and his family had been there on multiple occasions. Paige had noticed. Plus, she'd told her story countless times, to the police, FBI, Robin's parents, her parents, Dr. Swick, and on and on. Kaj wasn't merely asking because he was curious or nosy, but because he liked the girl who'd been taken. He was her boyfriend, if not officially, than very close to being.

"One minute everything was normal and then a door opened and it was never the same," Paige said. It was scary how easily she could go back to that night, jumping on Robin's bed—up and down, up and down.

"How did he get in?" Kaj asked.

Paige shook her head. "The police said the window. The FBI said he walked in through the back door."

"It was unlocked?"

Paige shrugged.

Kaj winced, saying, "Why'd it have to be unlocked." It was not a question but a statement.

Paige didn't know if she should tell him the next part of the story, the one that only Dr. Swick knew—not even her parents or sister knew. Why was she considering telling him? To absolve the guilt she carried with her throughout her days, throughout the past year?—guilt heavier than her backpack on the heaviest homework week. What might it have felt like to say the words to Kaj—to reveal the truth?

Paige was about to let the entire story tumble out but something stopped her. Some force of nature told her to keep her mouth shut.

"It's okay," Kaj said softly, breaking the silence.

She shook her head. "I'm sorry," she said.

Kaj shook his head. "You're so strong, Paige."

So strong? Ha! That was a laugh; that was the silliest thing she'd ever heard.

Kaj now looked as though he might cry. Paige hoped he wouldn't, mostly because she didn't know what she'd do, but it didn't matter because what he did instead was come over to the bed, put his arm around her, and place his lips right up to hers. Technically, this was her first kiss, although at the beginning of seventh grade she'd kissed Bruce on the stairs at Caroline's house. That had felt stiff and wooden, but this was something else—something more consuming, like hunger.

They both went from sitting on the bed to lying down. Kaj broke away from their kissing only to remove his glasses, which he tossed behind him, and the gesture made Paige giggle. Kaj probed her lips open with his tongue. She thought she might shriek in disgust; his tongue, wet like a snail poking around in her mouth, but instead she found she liked it and greeted it with her own tongue. She was breathing harder and he was rubbing her shoulder with his hand. He made a noise like *uuumph* and she answered with another guttural sound like *rrrnnmm*. She wondered if this is how he kissed Robin, and then wondered if he was thinking about her. How could he not be? They were both pressing their lips into the empty space that was now Robin. They stayed this way on the bed for ten, maybe fifteen minutes when suddenly her door swung open. It was Erin. Paige pulled away from Kaj.

"Oh?" Erin said, and slammed the door shut again.

"Uh oh," Kaj said.

Paige raised her eyebrows. She wanted more of Kaj and his tawny brown skin and slippery tongue. "It's okay," she assured him. "It was just my sister. I don't know why she's even home."

Tentatively they found their way back to each other. They shifted positions so their heads were now on pillows at the head of the bed and they could stretch out their legs instead of dangling them uncomfortably over the floor.

"Is this okay?" Kaj asked, but went back to kissing before she could answer *yes*.

Paige wrapped an arm around his waist and rubbed his lower back the way he was rubbing her shoulder. They pulled apart only to look at each other, and when their lips remet Paige slipped her hand under his blue oxford shirt and felt the skin of his back on her fingers. He did the same to her and pulled her in even closer.

The door opened again, without a warning. "What's going on in here?" It was her mother, stern and commanding.

They rolled apart from each other as soon as they heard the door. Kaj fumbled for his glasses, which were now at the foot of the bed.

"We're doing homework," Paige said. She could feel the ghost of his fingers tickling her back, and her breath still came quick and shallow.

"I think it's time for . . . ," her mom pointed toward Kaj without saying his name.

"Kaj," Paige said. "You know Kaj."

"To have Kag's mother come pick him up," she said.

"It's pronounced *Kai*," Paige said, and when she did, he smiled at her, his glasses now a little crooked on his face.

Every action had the consequence of a family meeting. When Paige quit volleyball . . . *family meeting*, when Paige moved back into her own bedroom . . . *family meeting*. And now Paige's first make-out session . . . *family meeting*.

They sat in the living room the next evening.

"In the future," her dad said, "if you have a boy in the house, you must keep your door open."

"No," her mom corrected. "You must stay downstairs. No boys in your room, period."

Paige didn't know why but she laughed.

"It's funny?" her mom said. "It's not funny. You're lucky we're not punishing you for a month. Dr. Swick said—"

"You spoke to Dr. Swick?"

"Absolutely. You bet we did," her mom said.

Paige turned to her dad but he wouldn't meet her gaze—the same way she wouldn't meet Erin's.

"Great," Paige said. "So now the whole world knows about this?"

"Not the whole world," her mom said, shaking her head.

"Are we done?" Paige asked.

"We're not," her dad said.

Paige slumped in the chair.

"We want to know what you were thinking," her dad said in a gentle tone, looking at her mom and then at Erin.

Paige shrugged. She wondered if Kaj and his parents were sitting in their own living room having the same, horrible conversation. Paige shook her head. "I've known Kaj since I was ten," she said. She thought about it, redid the math. "No, eight," she said. "He's hardly a stranger."

"We're just concerned, is all," her dad said. "It's not *like* you to have a boy over. You didn't even ask us if it was okay."

Paige needed the family meeting to be over. Why did everything in her life have to play out so publically? "Sorry," she finally said, hoping that could be the beginning of the end of it.

"Can I say something?" Erin asked.

Paige looked to the floor.

"Of course," her dad said.

"Paige is obviously mad at me but I don't think she realizes what I was thinking when I saw them. I didn't know who he was. I didn't know if she was in trouble or not. I didn't know what was happening. I'm not the bad guy here," she said. "I was just worried."

Paige studied the grains of wood in the floor.

"Did you hear your sister?" her mom said.

Paige shook her head.

"Could you acknowledge her?" her mom said.

Paige looked up. "Hi," she said to Erin.

Her dad said, "Acknowledge what she *said*, smarty pants."

"I heard you," she said to Erin.

"I wasn't telling on you. I was *scared* for you. Seriously," Erin said.

"I heard you," Paige said again. Okay, were they done talking about her first real kiss . . . with tongue . . . and a shoulder caress?

When her dad said, "There's something else," Paige thought she might explode.

"It's a good 'something else,'" Erin chimed in.

Paige looked toward her mom, who had softened and was now smiling in earnest. "We've decided you can get a cat," she said.

"A kitten," Erin corrected.

"I can?"

"But it's going to be your responsibility," her dad said. "You're dealing with the litter box and feeding it."

"I'll help," Erin said, under her breath.

"You're serious?" Paige said to her mom.

"We're serious," she said back.

This was the best mixed message she'd received all day. She wondered if she could get a puppy if she brought another guy up to her room.

"We can go to the shelter this weekend," her dad said.

It was only Wednesday. "Why can't we go now?" Paige whined.

Her dad gazed at his watch. "I don't think they're open. It's almost dinnertime."

Erin jumped up. "I'll find out," she said, running to the phone in the kitchen.

"Thank you so much," Paige said to her parents.

"You can thank Dr. Swick when you see him on Monday," her mom said.

She wondered when that phone call took place—sometime between her mom walking in on them and this family meeting, almost twenty-four hours later. Dr. Swick was an integral part of their lives now, and it wasn't the worst thing. Paige appreciated going to his office once a week in Marin. She felt heard by him in a way she didn't feel heard by others. He listened and responded to her in a calm, even way, not in the frantic way her family responded.

Erin came back into the room, disappointed. "They close at six," she said.

"We'll go Friday," her dad said. "Okay?"

Paige didn't quite know how she'd wait until then.

For the first time in a long time, Paige was excited to get to school. She put on a white skirt and red sweater instead of her regular jeans and a boxy T-shirt, and even ran a brush through her tangled, brown hair. "Don't you look nice," her mom said as she slipped out the front door. She didn't have any classes with Kaj this semester but she was sure she'd at least see him at lunch. In her fantasy last night, she pictured the following conversation unfolding:

Kaj: Sorry about yesterday.

Paige: Want to come over? My parents are out for the evening.

Kaj: Yeah. You bet I do.

Paige: Great. We can continue where we left off.

Kaj: I'd love that.

She finally ran into him at the water fountain between classes. It wasn't a run-in necessarily; she'd seen him from a distance and joined the long line for the fountain. Why was everyone so thirsty?

"Hi," she said, as he walked passed her, wiping his mouth.

"Hey," he said, raising his eyebrows and continuing along.

Paige was next for the water but she jumped out of line to join him. "Sorry about yesterday," she said, contriving a laugh, even though there was nothing really funny about it.

"Yeah," he said. "I don't think your mom wants anything to do with me!"

"No," Paige said. "It's not you. Everyone's just worried about me. It's totally annoying."

"Yeah," he said. "But I get it."

He didn't explain what part he *got*. He just smiled weakly and picked up the pace.

Paige followed. "I'm okay," Paige said.

"Well, see you later," Kaj said, lifting his hand into a half salute, which looked to Paige like he was shielding himself from her.

"No," Paige said, a little too loudly. "I quit volleyball, remember?"

But he didn't seem to remember, or care, even. Had he gotten in trouble at home? Had his parents warned him about spending time with the girl from the scene of the crime?

Paige started to follow him, but then dropped back when she could no longer see him. She looked around at her classmates at their lockers, filing into classrooms, and wondered who else was keeping their distance from the girl who had a brush with evil.

Mrs. Singer stood in front of the class, a proud smile on her face. "Today, I'm bringing back the art of the letter." *The art of the letter*, Paige thought, disappointed. She was already well versed in the art of the letter, having exchanged at least twenty with Caroline this semester alone.

Mrs. Singer opened her desk drawer and retrieved a large pile of blue stationery. She walked around the class distributing two sheets per student. "This new age of e-mails is making your brains soggy," she said with a dramatic flourish. "Your assignment today is to fill both sheets of paper with a letter to anyone you so choose. Spelling counts. Neat handwriting counts."

Some students grumbled.

"It's my job to get you back on track," she said. "And I take my job very seriously."

Who would Paige write to? She owed her grandpa Joseph a letter, but probably couldn't fill two pages to him. How about a letter to Kaj, rewriting what had happened the other day? Paige searched her backpack for her favorite pen, the blue one with the felt tip. She aligned the stationery, one on top of the other, and very suddenly realized who needed to hear from her. She set the pen to the paper and started the letter.

To David Bradley Lancaster,
 Last year I went on a field trip to Alcatraz and felt sorry for the prisoners. Their cells were so tiny and they had to sleep in the same space as their toilets. Ewww! I used to think prison was cruel and unusual punishment until you showed up in my best friend's bedroom— talk about cruel and unusual.

First of all, I'd like to know what made you think you could just walk into a stranger's house. No knock? No doorbell? You were born, unfortunately, so that must mean you had a mother and father at some point. Did they forget to teach you manners? Did you know you're supposed to chew with your mouth closed, and say please and thank you? Did you know that you're not supposed to kidnap, rape, and murder innocent twelve-year-old girls?

Why Robin? The friendliest, nicest, best friend I've ever known? The FBI said you were watching her from the park across the street. Did you follow her from her mom's to her dad's to her mom's again? Did you know that Briscoe lived with her dad and that's the reason you got her at her mom's?

I heard your trial is going to be next September and while the school year will be gearing up, you'll be sitting in a hot courtroom with all of Robin's family and friends, including me, staring at you. We will stab you with invisible daggers over and over again.

When I described you to the criminal sketch artist I forgot to mention how disgusting you smelled. I bet your parents didn't teach you about washing either, or that smoking and drinking are bad for you.

I was so excited when I heard they found you. You touched everything and left your stupid fingerprints on Robin's bed and dresser and door, you stupid idiot.

And when Caroline and I got dragged to the police station again—the third time in two weeks—we were both giddy with hope that you had spared our best friend, and yet shaking in fear of seeing your ugly face again. When they marched you and the parade of other hideous criminals out, you stood behind the double glass and even though my parents taught me it was rude to point, I stuck my finger out at you and yelled, "Him, that's him for sure!" and Caroline cried and pointed, too. You looked so pathetic. A dumb criminal caught—by two twelve-year-olds. Did you really think you could get away with murder? I don't think I'll ever understand why you crossed our paths, but your mere existence ruined our lives. Wherever you end up, I hope you rot there.

When Paige finally dropped the pen, her fingers tight and achy from writing, she looked around and realized she was the only one left in the classroom, except for Mrs. Singer who was sitting at her desk reading through some of the letters. "You finished?" she asked.

"Yes," Paige said.

"I look forward to reading it," she said. "You were writing so passionately."

This was a problem because Paige wasn't ready for anyone to see it. "Do I have to turn it in?" she asked.

"It was your assignment," Mrs. Singer said, standing up and walking toward her.

Paige quickly folded the pages and slipped them into her backpack. "I can't," she said.

Mrs. Singer stood in front of her. "I'm the only one who will see it," she assured her.

Paige shook her head no.

Mrs. Singer asked kindly, "Is it a letter to Robin?"

Paige didn't want to lie, so she didn't say yes, just nodded vaguely up and down and a little round and round.

"I understand," Mrs. Singer said, sighing. "You've been through so much, poor thing."

Paige didn't see herself as a "poor thing." She was alive, breathing, going to school. The "thing" was David Bradley Lancaster, the one sleeping in the same room as his toilet.

When she arrived home after school, Paige ran upstairs and slipped the letter into a white envelope, sealing it. What if she mailed it? Stuck a stamp on it and dropped it into the post box? She pictured him in prison, excited to be receiving a letter in his cell, and then she pictured him reading it, steam coming out of his ears like an angry cartoon. He would be locked up, but what if, just what if, he got out by some twist of fate—a prison escape or a powerful earthquake that knocked over the building. Would he dare come back to town and go after her? Hunt Paige down and drag her to the woods, to the same fate as Robin? The thought made her shudder. She shoved the envelope into her desk drawer and headed into Erin's room to use the computer.

When she typed *San Quintin* into the search engine, because that's where everyone said he'd go after the trial, a message appeared asking of she meant *San Quentin State Prison* and she clicked on the correct spelling, which took her to a home page with an aerial picture of the compound, on water like Alcatraz. She studied the image. He would be in there, that killer, somewhere in one of those cinder-block buildings, so she wrote the address down on the inside of her palm and then back in her room transcribed it on to the envelope. *David Bradley Lancaster.* Such a long name for such a nonperson. She went into the bathroom and scrubbed with soap until the ink bled down the drain and her hands were finally clean. She crawled into bed, even though it was still day, surprised that her pillow still smelled faintly of Kaj.

Paige and her dad drove fifteen minutes to the local animal shelter. Paige had dreamed about this moment for as long as she could remember. The car ride was charged with enthusiasm, but upon entering the premises, she experienced that feeling of leaking energy that had become all too familiar to her recently.

The dogs and cats were in separate spaces and though she was curious to at least see the dogs, she chose to enter the cat area. Cages were lined up and piled on top of each other and sometimes there were four cats per cage. Some were meowing, others howling. As they strolled down the aisles, oohing and ahhing over various names and breeds, some actually reached their paws out from behind the bars. There was no denying that the place looked like kitty jail and just like that Paige's mind slipped to thoughts about the intruder and how he was locked up in jail, too, waiting for a trial, only he had committed an unspeakable crime and these cats, all twenty, thirty, forty of them, had done absolutely nothing wrong. Their only crime was that they'd been born. How was it fair that they were in here and that Robin was. . . .

"You like that one?" her dad said. She'd stopped at a cage and it probably looked like she was watching a cat, but she was miles away. Her dad's voice snapped her back and when she focused she saw two gray tabby kittens, one sleeping in the litter box and the other swatting at Paige.

"I want them," Paige said. She had to get out of this prison as soon as possible.

"Them?" her dad said. "We didn't say you could get two."

The woman working there approached when she heard the conversation. "Just so you know," she said to Paige's dad, "we always encourage people to adopt two."

Her dad looked concerned.

"It's better for the animals, plus these two are brother and sister," she said. "You don't want to separate them. They're around seven months old, old enough so you won't have to deal with real kitteny things, like accidents or chewing." She unhinged the prison door. "Adam and Eve," she said, reaching for the one in the litter box. She wrapped her hand around the little fur ball, brushed him off, and handed him to Paige's dad, who looked totally bewildered holding a kitten. She passed the other one, Eve, to Paige. The soft fur immediately calmed her. She scratched around its ears. The cat clung to her blue-jean jacket and looked her in the eyes. It wasn't love at first sight but it would do. Anything to get out of here.

"You don't want to look around some more?" her dad said, still holding Adam. They'd been in the shelter no more than ten minutes.

"Nope," Paige said.

Her dad sighed. "So we're getting two," he said.

Paige smiled at him, a thank-you grin. She was grateful she was here with him and him only. Erin would have wanted to visit with every animal, and her mom most likely wouldn't allow two cats. Finally, this was the wish that Robin had granted her last year. She winced at the irony.

Back at the house, after a cursory explanation about why they had brought home more than one, her family set up an area in Paige's room and watched the kittens pounce, play, chase, groom, and explore. Erin thought their names were too somber. "Who wants animals named after biblical characters?" she said, and so they brainstormed others until they settled on Lucy and Desi—perfect, since the cats added much-needed levity to the household.

One morning, not long after Paige quit the volleyball team and got a C– on a math test on which she should have gotten an A, she woke and simply could not get out of bed. She wasn't tired, really, more like leaden, heavy, a dead weight. When her alarm sounded, she hit the snooze button, and after a few minutes when the music started up, she hit snooze again. Desi nipped at her toes, but she swatted him away. Erin poked her head through the bathroom door. "It's almost eight," she said insistently.

"I know," Paige said, and even her words came out heavy, like syrup.

A few minutes later her mom appeared at the door, dressed for work. "Are you feeling sick?" she asked, cautiously.

She wasn't sick the way she knew sick—no coughing or nausea or stuffiness. Her mom came closer and peered down at Paige who was still immobile on the bed. "You want to stay home today?"

It took too much energy even to nod yes. Her mom put her hand on Paige's forehead and smoothed it over her hair.

"Is she okay?" Erin called from the bathroom.

Paige smiled weakly.

"She's going to take the day off," her mom said. And then to Paige, "I'm going to, too."

Paige was perfectly fine staying home alone in bed; her mom would only be six blocks away at Infinitea but she couldn't muster the strength to express the thought. That, plus never in a million years would she be allowed to stay home alone. It was only when her mom said, "Dr. Swick warned us there would be days like this," that Paige realized it was November 10, a year to the day since Robin's body was found. She knew then that she was suffering from a sickness of the spirit, not a virus.

Her mom didn't leave her. She changed into a gray tracksuit, read the paper downstairs, and brought tea up to Paige, who left her bed only to use the bathroom.

Back in bed, Paige thought about the day, a little over a year ago, that she and Caroline and their families went to police headquarters to meet a prominent sketch artist, not like the one who showed up at Robin's house hours after her abduction and just asked for the basics—height, weight, age, hair, and eye color.

Since they were the only two who'd seen the intruder, they were the ones responsible for getting his image out to the media. The new artist was a woman named Jolie and she engaged them in real conversation. She didn't ask about height, weight, and age. Instead, she wanted to know what their favorite subjects were at school, what they watched on TV, if the intruder was an animal what would he be.

"A walrus," Paige said.

"A squirrel," Caroline said. "His cheeks were fat."

"But he was big like a walrus," Paige said.

Who were their favorite teachers? Where the last place their families went on vacation? What was the intruder's most prominent feature?

"His hands," Caroline said. "They were massively huge."

"His eyes," Paige said.

"Why's that?" Jolie asked.

"Because they were black."

Jolie adjusted her drawings as they spoke. She erased certain parts with a round, gray eraser. Her hand moved as though she were petting a cat.

"I wish *he* could speak," Paige said, referring to the stuffed bear she was clutching. "He saw everything."

"Is that your bear?" Jolie asked.

"Its Robin's," Caroline explained. "That one's Cinnamon, and this one's Rodney," she said referring to the one on her own lap. "We're taking care of them until she comes home."

"We're fostering them," Paige said.

"What would Cinnamon tell me about that night?" Jolie asked.

Caroline looked at Paige who said, "He'd say he was scared to death and he wanted to scream but he couldn't because he doesn't have a voice."

After an hour and a half, Jolie presented the girls with three sketches and both immediately pointed to the one in the middle. "That's him, but his cheeks were even fatter," Caroline said, and Jolie took her charcoal to the paper and added weight to his face. Paige felt a little sick as she watched the drawing inflate to reveal the man she'd encountered, the man who'd snatched Robin.

"Would you girls like some water?" a police officer, the cute one, asked. Caroline said no as Paige said yes. "You've been an enormous help today," he said, handing Paige a paper cup.

"Do you think they'll find her?" Caroline asked.

"We're one step closer than we were an hour ago," he said.

Upon hearing this, drinking the water, and completing the awful task of re-creating that ugly face, Paige felt her first stirrings of hope since the whole ordeal had begun.

Greeting Caroline and Paige in the lobby were their families, their brows knit in perpetual worry since learning their daughters had narrowly escaped a kidnapping. Paige's dad folded her into his arms and Paige watched as Caroline's dad did the same. "You did good," Caroline's dad said to his daughter.

"We're going to find her, kiddo," Paige's dad said, leading her out of the police station.

As they exited, they were met by a swarm of cameras, and the energy suddenly felt electric and even more hopeful. Strangers called to them by name.

"Caroline, Paige, do you have any messages for Robin?"

"Come home safely," Caroline said.

"Caroline, Paige, were you able to give an accurate description of the kidnapper?" Caroline clutched her bear and with the other hand gave a thumbs-up, and Paige took her lead and did the same.

The next day that image of them was splashed across papers everywhere—the front page of their local paper, the *San Francisco Chronicle*, *The Sacramento Bee*, even the *Portland Tribune*. Robin's disappearance wasn't front-page news in New York, but the photo still made the *Times*, albeit a few pages in. That day they were so sure they were going to return those bears to Robin. Hope was visible in that photo. It was the last photograph in which Paige recognized herself.

In the afternoon Erin came home, and her dad arrived early in the evening. Paige managed to make it downstairs for dinner, still in her pajamas. She brought Cinnamon down, too, and held him on her lap as she ate a baked potato with sour cream and chives. Upstairs, back in bed, her stomach churning, she pulled the bear's face close to hers and inhaled deeply. She couldn't understand how or why but over a year later, it still smelled like Robin's room—it still smelled like Robin.

On New Year's Eve they sat in the den as a family, Paige and Erin with sparkling apple juice and their parents with the real bubbly. Erin wanted to go to a party; Paige overheard a muffled conversation behind closed doors of her parents' bedroom earlier that week. Their mother had spoken in a clear and stern tone as she explained to Erin how important it was to be together as a family this year.

"But all my friends are going. Pleeease, Mom?"

"I'm positive your friends will understand."

"Can't I have dinner here and then go with them later?"

Paige heard her mom say "No."

Erin tried again. "What if I discuss it with Paige?"

Her mom raised her voice. "You're not hearing me. Dr. Swick said it was crucial to be together as a family."

"But you said that last year."

"Yes, and I'm saying it again."

"So I'm stuck here every New Year's Eve? For, what, the rest of my life?"

Paige felt badly. She thought about walking in and releasing Erin of her family obligations. She hoped Erin wouldn't blame her for her screwed up social life.

"It's part of your sister's recovery," her mom said. "And I'm not discussing it anymore."

So there they were on that Friday night, celebrating as a family, which meant watching Dick Clark as he announced various bands that to Paige all seemed to blur into one. Brandi someone or was it Brady? And a blonde girl who looked about Paige's age, a skirt hitched up high as she stomped around the stage.

They played Scrabble and ate Chinese food, and as it neared midnight the camera panned to the crowds in Times Square, bundled tight in winter clothes but charged with enthusiasm. People were jumping up and down, waving flags, kissing. There was so much excitement in the air and yet the only feeling Paige could muster was that of sorrow. It would be Saturday tomorrow, a new month, a new year, inching closer to a new century, even. Paige didn't want to move forward. If anything she wanted to move back, jump through the television screen and tackle Dick Clark. She wanted to lift the dropping ball, fly it back to the top like she imagined

Superman or Hercules might. The only thing she wanted, as the year came to an official end, was to turn back the hands of time. How could anyone look forward to a future without Robin?

Seventh Grade

The beginning-of-the-school-year party was held at Caroline's house because it was big and her parents always offered it up for parties. Bruce came in like a cyclone, slamming up against everyone. He grabbed girls on the dance floor and spun them around. Paige purposely jumped into his field of vision, and when he saw her he grabbed her onto the dance floor, and they whirled around the room crashing into people, spilling drinks and laughing. "Jitterbug!" Bruce screamed apropos of nothing and flailed his arms around and knocked his knees together. Paige tried to keep up but she looked more like a dopey marionette.

When the song ended, Paige searched for Caroline and finally found her in the kitchen. "What are you and Bruce doing?" Caroline said. "You got soda all over the floor."

"Sorry," Paige said. "We were just having fun."

"I don't get him," Caroline said. "He's so annoying and you just get swept up in it. You're like clowns together."

Paige followed her out of the kitchen and to the living room floor where she wiped up some ginger ale. "Aww," Caroline said, noticing something. "Now *that's* cute."

Paige looked up and saw Robin and Kaj slow dancing. Robin's head was leaning into Kaj's scrawny shoulder—she was so little and fit into his body the way a bird might tuck itself into its mother.

"See, that would never happen with Bruce," Caroline said.

Paige was fine with that. She didn't want that to happen. She liked the way things were.

Robin lifted her head off of Kaj's shoulder for an instant and noticed her friends watching. She looked soft and dreamy, a little glazed.

"Oh my God, where's my camera?" Caroline said.

"No!" Paige said. "You'll embarrass her!"

"She'll so want a picture of them dancing. Trust me." Caroline headed back into the kitchen.

Holding Robin, Kaj looked like he was concentrating really hard—thinking about a math problem or how to spell a certain word. The song ended and a faster one began. Robin and Kaj walked out of the room, hand in hand, just as Caroline returned with the camera.

"You missed it," Paige said.

Out of nowhere, Bruce ran up and pushed his face in close to Paige's. "Take our picture," he insisted.

Caroline rolled her eyes. "I wouldn't want to break the camera."

Upstairs, Paige fished for her camera in her overnight bag which was on Caroline's bed. She hadn't noticed before, but there was also a book on the bed, *What's Happening to My Body?* Paige stopped her search and instead flipped through the pages, whizzing past developing breasts and dangling penises and a few ram-shaped diagrams explaining how ovaries worked. It was like a comic book with exaggerated pictures and funny dialogue. Paige landed on the chapter titled, "Some Slang Words for the Penis and Testicles" and read, "schlong, wee-wee, wanger, tool, frankfurter, thing."

"I knew you'd be in here looking at this," Caroline said, snatching the book out of her hand.

"I was just looking for my camera," Paige said, embarrassed.

Caroline read from where Paige had left off, "Frankfurter, thing, dick, dong, penie, dinky."

"I can't believe they're allowed to write that in a book," Paige said.

"A book my mom bought me!" Caroline said. "Hey, you didn't hear it from me, but Beth got her period." She slammed the book shut and threw it back onto her bed.

"What? How do you know?"

"How do you think?" Caroline said. "She told me. She said she went out for Italian food with her family and when she got home she got it and she said to her mom, 'I think the pizza sauce came out the other end.'"

"Why would she say that?"

"I thought it was kind of funny," Caroline said.

Paige said, "She didn't really think it was the pizza sauce, did she?"

"I think she was just trying to be funny," Caroline said.

Paige didn't understand how anything involving bloody eggs could be funny. Whereas Caroline couldn't wait to get hers, Paige was perfectly fine as things were now, period-free. Once when she was in fifth grade she'd noticed a package of pads appear in the cabinet under the sink in the bathroom she and her sister shared. Curious, she dug into the open package and extracted a thick pad wrapped in yellow casing. It was folded in thirds. She pulled it out, peeled off the backing, and affixed it to her underwear, as she presumed it was supposed to be worn. It felt thick and bulky between her legs, like a concentrated diaper and it made a crinkling noise when she walked. She stood in front of the full-length bathroom mirror, at first in her underwear, looking like she had a penis, and then in her jeans, which masked the bulk only a little. Uch, this was the last thing she wanted to deal with and wondered how long her sister had been in this prison. Paige ripped the pad off her underwear and tossed it into the toilet before flushing. Later, when the toilet clogged and the plumber was called to fix it, she was caught, her curiosity now public knowledge. She had to endure a cringeworthy lecture from her mom about never throwing pads down the toilet bowl; the whole time Erin glared at her in contempt.

"Okay, come back to the party," Caroline said, tugging on Paige's arm.

"One sec," Paige said. "I just want to get my camera."

But when Caroline left the room and Paige was sure she was alone, she reopened the book on puberty and turned to the page of the penis—first a boy's size and then a man's. She studied the drawing of an erection, intrigued and disgusted at the way it could lift and point.

On her way downstairs, Paige thought she heard noise coming from Kenny's room. She turned around and approached his door, nudging it open. It was dark but Paige could see two bodies on the water bed. She flicked on the light switch and watched as Kaj and Robin pulled apart. Robin's lips were puffy.

"What are you doing?" Robin said, squinting.

"What are *you* doing?" Paige said.

"We're just hanging out," Kaj said, sitting up. The water bed sloshed around beneath him, giving Kaj a little ride.

Robin giggled.

"There's a party downstairs," Paige said, "just so you know."

"Yeah," Kaj said. "We know."

Paige was burning with jealousy—not because of Kaj, necessarily, but because Robin was making out, something Paige had never done before, on a water bed, no less. Robin raised an eyebrow, indicating that Paige should leave.

"No," Paige said, which seemed to embarrass Robin even more.

"What's up?" Kaj said.

Paige couldn't help herself. She glanced between Kaj's legs to see if anything there was pointing up.

"Nothing," she said.

Robin crawled over to where Kaj was sitting, the bed rippling along with her. When the girls spent the night at Caroline's, that's the room they always slept in—three of them sloshing around on the too-big bed. Something felt ruined now. Robin had moved forward in a direction that could never be reversed.

"Were you just coming to say hi?" Robin asked.

"I heard a noise. I was investigating."

"Did you think it was the bogeyman?" Robin said waving her fingers around and laughing.

Kaj stood up and walked to the closet door, opening it he said, "Oops, where's the bathroom?"

"Not in there," Paige said, laughing.

"To the right, then to the left," Robin indicated, and Kaj walked out of the bedroom.

A silence fell between them, and Paige wanted to fill it but she couldn't find anything to say. The water in the bed glugged every time Robin moved. Muted party sounds rose from downstairs. "So, is Kaj, like, your boyfriend now or something?" Paige finally asked, nervous to hear the answer.

Robin shrugged. "What does that even mean?" she said.

"Boyfriend?" Paige clarified, "*Special friend.*"

"I like him," Robin said. "He likes me. But I wouldn't call him my boyfriend."

"Why not?" Paige asked.

"I don't know. This is the first time we ever even kissed," she said. "Maybe by Christmas he'll be my boyfriend."

"I'm never gonna get a boyfriend," Paige said.

"Shut up," Robin said. "Yes you are. This is gonna be the best year ever."

"Paging Paige," Caroline called from downstairs. "Come in, Paige."

"Please don't say anything," Robin begged. "I'm not in the mood for her know-it-all-ness."

"Promise," Paige said, flashing the peace sign to Robin. "Coming!" she called, bumping into Kaj on her way out the door.

Back downstairs Paige noticed that the party had thinned to a final handful of guests. She was restless, bored, itching to stir up some sort of excitement. Paige poked her head into the living room and found Caroline and Gus on the dance floor. Great, now both of her best friends were occupied with boys. Caroline was at least two heads taller than Gus, yet she rested on his shoulder as Seal's "Kiss From a Rose" played. Suddenly, Bruce popped out of nowhere.

"You're still here?" Paige said.

"Yeah," he said, "but it's kind of boring. Everyone's paired off but us."

Before she could say anything, he leaned in to her, closed his eyes and puckered up. It felt like a weird place for a first kiss, on the landing of the stairs, lights on everywhere, Robin and Kaj just above them, Caroline and Gus right there in the living room, and Mr. and Mrs. Kershaw God knows where. Paige closed her eyes, too, and their lips met, tight and pursed. They dangled there for a few moments, his nose squishing hers. This was kissing? This was the big frigging deal? How long were they supposed to hold it? Bruce was the first to pull away. "I can't breathe," he said.

Paige laughed. "Me neither."

"Let's blow spitballs at Gus," he suggested, and Paige led him into the kitchen to look for straws.

A week after school started, Paige and her classmates took a trip to Alcatraz. They met at school at seven in the morning and drove the half hour into the city where they were to catch the nine o'clock ferry from Pier 33. When Robin didn't show up at school, Paige became worried. "We can't leave without her," she told Mrs. Segal, the history teacher who was doing the head count.

"I'm afraid we must," she said. "We've got a boat to catch."

And as the bus pulled away Paige kept her face pressed to the window, scanning the streets for any signs of Mrs. Hecht's white station wagon.

Robin turned up half an hour later at Pier 33, sweating and out of breath.

"What happened?" Paige said when they finally reunited on the upper deck.

"Uch," Robin said. "It's a long story."

"Your mom's always late," Caroline said.

Robin rolled her eyes and in an uncharacteristic tone said, "What do you know about my mom?"

"That she's always late," Caroline said.

Robin stomped her foot in frustration.

"You guys!" Paige said. "Just stop. You made it, that's all that matters."

Paige knew Robin's parents didn't get along, even before their divorce last year; it was obvious, like when Robin's mom showed up late for their fifth-grade chorus recital and her dad, already there, yelled at her above the music. "Can you *ever* get *anywhere* on time?" Or at Robin's house where they'd bicker furiously and Robin wouldn't even seem to notice. When her parents' divorce was finalized, Robin suddenly had two homes, with two bedrooms, two toothbrushes, and two phone numbers. Sometimes, Paige would be happy to get back home to her own quiet family— where her parents called each other "babe" and occasionally kissed over the kitchen table when passing the salt.

When they arrived at the island, Paige and Caroline stood behind a tired Robin and pushed her up the steep incline toward Alcatraz as Bruce and Gus ran by taunting them.

Once inside, everyone hooked up to their audio tours and explored the prison. Paige was struck by the injustice of it: how the criminals—Al Capone, George "Machine Gun"

Kelly, and "The Birdman" Robert Stroud—were stuck on the windy, desolate island, with sounds of the city wafting past. She was surprised at the sympathy she felt for them, their tiny cells, smaller than her bathroom, her closet, even, room only for a bed and a toilet. The building was dank and moldy.

The tour guided her to the solitary-confinement cells, where Caroline, Robin, Bruce, and Gus were laughing and taking pictures. "Let me out!" Robin said, rattling the bars, "I'm innocent!"

Bruce joined her in the cell. "Hey," he joked, "this is *my* solitary confinement, go find your own!" But Paige couldn't stand it—the claustrophobic cell, the musty smell. She followed the tour to another part of the prison and there found herself rooting for the prisoners as the narrator spoke of the escape attempts. So desperate to get out, some prisoners dug through the walls with spoons from the dining hall and escaped to the roof, climbing the pipes behind the walls. Paige thought to herself, *yes!* She found it so inventive and it only proved how desperately they wanted out.

At the end of the tour, they returned their headsets, visited the gift shop, and headed outside to walk around the property.

"Escaped prisoner!" Bruce called as he ran by the girls at lightning speed. "Come arrest me!"

Paige started to go after him but Caroline pulled her back by the hood of her jacket.

"Ow!"

"Don't enable him," Caroline said.

They walked toward the gardens. The wind howled. Paige zipped up her jacket and covered her head with the hood. "I kind of feel sorry for the prisoners," she admitted.

"Why?" Caroline said.

"This!" Paige said, pointing to the grounds. "It's so cold and windy and far away."

"They deserved it," Caroline said. "Don't rob a bank if you don't want to end up here."

But Paige didn't think it was that simple.

"Hey, look!" Robin said. She was standing in front of some new flowers protected from the birds and elements by metal barbed wire. She took a picture. "Even the flowers are behind bars."

Paige was usually too busy for television, but on Thursday nights she cuddled up with her mom as they watched *Friends* together. Paige thought Rachel was so pretty and Phoebe made her laugh out loud, but her mom had a thing for Chandler. "He's got the best lines, hands down, every episode." Paige didn't always understand the innuendos, or why the audience would scream with laughter when Joey messed up another date and ended up on the couch alone, but she did hope Rachel and Ross would fall in love.

Tonight's episode revolved around Ross and Rachel getting into a fight about Ross's new girlfriend. At a commercial break, Paige asked if she could sleep at Robin's the next night.

"Again?" her mom said. "Weren't you just there last weekend?"

"That was Caroline's," Paige reminded her.

"Is it so bad here," her mom asked, "that you have to go away every weekend?"

"Pleeease?" Paige mugged, inching closer and closer to her mom, killing her with cuteness.

Her mom finally said. "Yes. You can sleep there."

Paige showered her with kisses. "Thank you, thank you, thank you," she said.

The show started again. The friends were in Central Perk discussing Ross's new girlfriend. Paige tried her luck with one more thing. "Can I get a cat?"

"Shhh," her mom said. "I can't hear Chandler."

Robin was staying at her mom's for the weekend. When Paige's mom dropped her off, Paige blew air-kisses before slamming the car door shut. "What time tomorrow?" her mom called out.

"I'll let you know later," Paige said, waving.

Her mom nodded in agreement.

"Don't you think it's time to retire the bears?" Caroline said, pushing all of Robin's stuffed animals to the side so she could get comfortable on her bed. "Especially now that you have a boyfriend?"

"I don't have a boyfriend!" Robin said, running to their rescue. "Do I?" The three of them burst out laughing.

Kaj and Robin had been eating their lunch together lately, away from the benches where everyone else convened. Paige still sat with Caroline, Beth, and Debbie but kept watch on Robin. *How did they have so much to talk about?* she wondered.

"You're asking us if you have a boyfriend?" Caroline said.

"I mean, what does it even mean to have a *boyfriend*," Robin said, mocking the word.

"It means you spend your lunch with him, which you do, it means you write his name in your notebook, which you do, it means he buys your presents, which he does," Caroline said.

Knowing she collected teddy bears, Kaj bought Robin a little red one that could fit inside her palm. She named him "Berry," because he was red like a berry, and of course because he was a bear.

"I just got rid of all my Barbies," Caroline said. "I gave them to The Salvation Army."

"Even Rollerblade Barbie?" Paige asked.

"She was the first to go."

Paige wished Caroline had given them to her instead.

"Hello?" Caroline said. "We're in seventh grade. We can't be playing with Barbies and teddy bears anymore."

"Just because you're giving away your childhood doesn't mean we have to," Paige said dramatically.

"I look at it as clearing the path for the next phase of life," Caroline said.

"Which is what?"

"Growing up," Caroline said. "Not lugging around teddy bears and Barbies."

"Was that something you read about in your puberty book?" Paige asked.

Caroline was growing frustrated. "You can do what you want with Cinnamon and Rodney," she said to Robin, waving toward the pack of stuffed bears on the bed. "Bring them to show-and-tell for all I care."

"There's no show-and-tell in seventh grade!" Paige said.

"That's exactly my point!" Caroline explained.

"I'm never getting rid of my bears," Robin said, joining them on the bed. "These guys are coming to college with me." She picked up Cinnamon and hugged him close.

Caroline said, "Well I guess you can practice kissing on him. You know. For Kaj."

"Eeeeew!" Paige said.

"I like him," Robin reminded her.

"Sorry," Paige said.

Robin put the bear down and walked to the closet. She pulled out a board game, *SweetHearts*.

"You really want to play that?" Caroline lamented.

"I really do," Robin said.

She set up the board and shuffled the deck of cards, each with a guy and his various stats: Bram, five feet ten, green eyes, loves basketball, coffee shops, and traveling. The object of the game was to collect as many sweethearts as possible before choosing your steady—then you cycled through a series of events to test if you chose the right guy for you.

While Robin was setting up, Paige swiped one of the cards and surreptitiously crossed out *Scott* and wrote in *Kaj*. Under the "Loves" heading, she replaced "horseback riding, rainy days, and dogs" with "tennis, math, and Robin," and slid it back into the deck. But once they had begun the game it was Caroline who picked it. "Ha, ha, ha," she laughed mockingly and slapped the card down in front of Robin. "We have a comedienne in our presence."

Paige found a small rubber ball and threw it against Robin's wall, catching it on the rebound. "I can't wait till Halloween," she said, throwing and catching it again.

"Are we going in my neighborhood this year?" Caroline asked.

"What do you mean *this year*?" Robin said. "We go in your neighborhood every year."

"It's not my fault that's where the best haunted houses are."

Suddenly the door swung open. "Girls!" Robin's mom said. "Do you understand how exhausted I am?" The noise startled Paige and she missed catching the ball. It rolled into the bathroom. "Do you?" her mom pressed. No one answered. "What is that God awful noise?" she asked. No one said anything, though Paige assumed she meant the thumping of the ball against the wall. "For the last time . . .

Keep. It. Down." And with that she pivoted on her heels, leaving the room in a huff.

"Someone needs to take a chill pill," Caroline said when she was out of earshot.

"She gets like that when she has migraines," Robin defended.

Caroline rolled her eyes and Paige knew what she was thinking, *no wonder her parents got divorced.* "She always has migraines," Caroline said. "Don't you think she should see a doctor or something?"

Later, they stood in Robin's bathroom all playing with a bag full of makeup and trying on their Halloween costumes. They decided they were all going to be genies this year. Robin applied an orange lipstick. "I think I'm going to wear this one."

"Cool," Caroline said, smacking her own ruby-red lips together. "Put the whole outfit on," she said. Robin did as she was told, and emerged in a shiny yellow getup, a red sash across her waist, and a beanie cap on her head.

"Awesome!" Caroline said.

"Make a wish," Paige said.

"No, I'm supposed to grant *you* the wish," Robin corrected. "What do you want?"

"Wish for me to get my period," Caroline said.

"Your wish is my command," she said, anointing her. "And you?" she said to Paige.

"I'd like a cat."

"Two more wishes," Robin said.

"Okay, two cats," Paige said.

"One more."

Paige thought for a minute. "World peace?"

Caroline laughed, "That's a tall order."

"Not as tall as two cats," Paige said.

The girls peeled out of their outfits. Robin stepped into a jumpsuit that was hanging over her chair while Caroline changed into her heart-themed pajamas.

Paige somersaulted onto Robin's bed.

"I wanna try," Robin said, taking a running leap onto her bed but miscalculating and smacking her feet against the wall with a thud. "Ow, ow, ow!" she bellowed. Paige collapsed into a heap of giggles.

They both made their way upright and started jumping on the bed. Paige reached out for Robin's hands, and they jumped like they were on a seesaw, up and down, up and down, breathy and giggling, the bed squeaking under their weight. Caroline, who had been in the bathroom brushing her teeth came out just as Robin's door swung open again and through it walked a man, burly and agitated.

He kicked the door closed behind him. "Who lives here?" he said, looking from one girl to the other. Paige dropped Robin's hand and looked at her imploringly. Robin's expression was that of alarm. But when Paige looked toward Caroline, she noticed a smirk on her face. It calmed her, seeing that grin. It was nothing like the look her grandmother had on the phone when she'd learned about her dad's mugging in Europe. What was going on here? Paige heard a *flick* and saw that the man, the fat lug, had a knife. "Who lives here?" he said in a gravelly voice. The room was starting to smell. It was not a smell Paige recognized, liquor, maybe? Sweat mixed with trash? Whatever it was, it was not nice. Caroline and Paige both looked toward Robin, maybe hoping for answers. The man approached and waved the knife at Paige. She'd never seen that kind of knife so close. It taunted her with its sharpness. She tried to blink him away. Her heart was beating fast from jumping, but now extra fast from the unknown. "Who lives here?" he said again, his coal eyes focused on Paige, his knife inching closer and closer to her stomach. She couldn't think straight, and she couldn't see, either, her vision had blurred and become unfocused. She swallowed hard. She barely lifted a finger as she pointed towards Robin. Caroline was still smirking but her eyebrows were furrowed. Before Paige could think to do anything else, scream perhaps, or make a run for the door, she was on the floor with Caroline, swept up by the stranger in one startling move.

Now they were on their stomachs because the intruder was tying up their arms and feet in thick, scratchy rope. Had a minute passed? Or maybe an hour? Paige started to shake and suddenly she felt herself going to the bathroom, urine running down her leg like a little girl. "Nobody make a noise," the voice said, hushed, and Paige started whimpering, a sound she'd never heard herself make before, a sound she didn't mean to make. Caroline was silent. "I'm just here for the valuables," the voice said again, only louder. And then, "Get me pillows." Paige gazed up, even though she was face down on the floor, she craned her neck and watched Robin approach her bed with the intruder's knife at her back. This couldn't be right. This couldn't be real. Robin tossed her bear Cinnamon to the side before handing two pillows to him, and he took them, stuffing them over Caroline's and Robin's heads. Paige could hear the muffled sounds of crying. She didn't know if it was Robin or Caroline. There was a humming noise, too, close to her ears and after a minute she deduced that it was the rush of her own blood coursing through her body. She could hear that and her heart *thump-thumping* against her chest. The rope scratched her wrists. Her arms were behind her and raised a little, like a swimmer mid butterfly stroke. Her shoulders ached. But she didn't hear the man anymore, and she didn't hear Robin. And she wondered when this nightmare would be over.

Sixth Grade

It was December and the girls were on Christmas break, which meant a flurry of slumber parties over the next few weeks. This year, none of their families were traveling anywhere, whereas last year Caroline's had gone to Paris and Robin's to New Orleans. Paige and Caroline slept at Robin's house the previous night, and in the morning Robin's mom bounded into the room and woke them up. "Daddy and I thought it would be a great day to go to the beach," she said.

Paige blinked open her eyes. Robin stirred.

"Honey?" Mrs. Hecht said.

"Okay," Paige said, though she knew she wasn't the "honey" her mom meant.

"Robin, honey," her mom said. "Your friends want to go to the beach, too."

Caroline stretched and rolled to her side. "What time is it?" she said in a gravelly, morning voice.

"Apparently it's time to go to the beach," Paige said.

"It's almost ten," Robin's mom said. "It's gorgeous out. Daddy's packing a picnic. C'mon, sleepyheads, the day is sneaking away!"

Robin's mom left the room, and a few seconds later Briscoe ran in, his nails clacking across the wood floor, eager to sniff everyone in sight. "Nooo!" Robin called as the dog jumped onto her bed.

"Briscoe!" Paige called, hoping he might roughhouse with her, but he only had eyes for Robin.

Robin's dad was an amateur photographer and he snapped a few photos of the girls as they climbed in to the backseat of the white Volvo wagon. "I have a fun idea," he said, as he stood in front of the backdoor waiting to close it. "I want to take a few pictures of you girls posed as letters of the alphabet, maybe for a children's book down the road. What do you think?" he asked. When no one answered, Paige said, "Cool!" She loved the idea, and didn't understand why Caroline rolled her eyes.

"Marjorie!" her dad called, as he stepped into the driver's seat, waiting for Mrs. Hecht to join them. He beeped his horn three times.

"Dad!" Robin said.

He beeped it a fourth time.

When Mrs. Hecht finally got into the car she said, "Sorry! I was trying to find the smoked Gouda." Mr. Hecht looked at them through the rearview mirror with an incredulous look on his face, which made Paige giggle.

They drove down the 101 Freeway, and Paige pressed her face against the window as they passed the sign for San Quentin State Prison. She pictured men in black-and-white striped uniforms with bombs attached to their ankles, as she'd seen in episodes of *Tom and Jerry*. "Did you know there's an adorable little town next to the prison?" Robin's mom said. "Michelle told me about it. She said it's absolutely the quaintest thing."

"Um, let's not find out," her dad said.

There was traffic on the Golden Gate Bridge, but Paige didn't mind. She loved looking out at the view from this perspective, the boats and ferries in the bay below, Alcatraz in the distance, and the views of San Francisco.

"*Gadda gan gadda gu gadda gask gadda gore gadda gad . . . ,*" Caroline said in rapid fire, "*gadda gange gadda gadation?*"

Robin obliged. "Dad, can you change the station?"

Robin's mom turned around. "It's the Giants game!" she said, looking at them. When nobody answered she said, "You girls with your private language . . . ," and switched it to a jazz station.

Robin's dad positioned them in the sand to form the letter A, with Robin completing the triangle. They were lopsided because Caroline was so much taller than they were. They worked better as B, with Paige and Robin curled against Caroline. "This is fantastic!" her dad said, standing above them with his camera. C and D worked fine, and for E, Caroline had to form an L with her long body as Paige and

Robin completed the other two bars. At G, Caroline bolted up from her curled position. "Can we please have a break?" she asked. "I'm dying of heat!" Paige was so glad she said something.

"You can't tough it out until K?" Robin's dad asked.

"Nooo!" Robin whined. "It's too hot!"

He finally relented, "We'll continue next week, okay?" he said, emphasizing the "k," which Paige found funny.

"Yeah, yeah," Caroline said dismissively.

When Briscoe ran over, Robin threw her arms around him. "Stay there," her dad said. "Don't let him leave," and took pictures of them from every angle. Paige had wanted her own dog since forever but her parents always said no. When she got home that night, she was going to try her luck again, but this time maybe ask for a cat, to ease them in.

The girls lay on their backs on the beach and stared up at the clouds. "Oh! Alligator!" Paige pointed, and then shouted, "dinosaur."

"Look!" Caroline said. "A king. Do you see the crown?"

"You're both so creative," Robin said. "I just see clouds."

Robin's parents were now sitting in a grassy area. Her mom was digging through the picnic basket, and her dad was tossing the ball to the dog. Robin said, "Let's walk to the water," and stood, pretending to walk a tightrope or a balance beam. The other girls followed, putting one foot in front of the other. The sand was soft and dry beneath Paige's feet and it warmed her from the inside. It soon became wet and firm as they reached the water's edge. The Golden Gate Bridge stood proudly to the right, and across from them the headlands seemed in arm's reach.

"Hey!" Robin's dad called, motioning *no* with his hand. "Don't go in!" There had been an ominous sign in the parking lot: PEOPLE SWIMMING AND WADING HAVE DROWNED HERE.

Robin turned toward him and, rolling her eyes, put her hand on her hip. "Dad," she called back. "As if!"

He gave her the okay sign and continued throwing the ball for Briscoe.

At that moment, a wave crashed just ahead of them, and they laughed at the spray of the water and ran back to the dry sand so as not to get too wet, so as not to get swept up by the tide.

Acknowledgements

Thank you to Crystal Patriarche for your enthusiasm and understanding regarding this project, Wayne Parrish for your precise and thoughtful edits, and Julie Metz for the poignant and perfect cover.

Thank you to the Can Serrat Artist Residency in El Bruc, Spain, which provided me with the time, space, and sustenance to complete this book.

Thank you to Michelle Kholos Brooks, Jennifer Caloyeras, Ron and Sheila Clark, Susan Gorton, Lisa Harper, Leena Pendharkar, Ruth Portner, David Rubenstein for early draft feedback.

I am grateful to everyone I met in Salt Lake City, Utah during the criminal trial for Elizabeth Smart's captor, especially the author Dorothy Allred Solomon.

About the Author

Melissa Clark is an author, television writer, and college instructor. She has written two previous novels: *Swimming Upstream, Slowly* and *Imperfect*. Her essay, "Rachael Ray Saved My Life," is included in the anthology *The Cassoulet Saved Our Marriage.* She is also the creator of the animated television series, *Braceface*, starring the voice of Alicia Silverstone, which aired on the ABC Family Channel. She has contributed scripts for *Rolie Polie Olie*, *Totally Spies*, and *Sweet Valley High*, among others. Melissa teaches creative writing and literature courses both privately and at Otis College of Art and Design in Los Angeles. Connect with the author on her website: www.melissaclarkwrites.com.

About SparkPress

SparkPress is an independent boutique publisher delivering high-quality, entertaining, and engaging content that enhances readers' lives, with a special focus on female-driven work. We are proud of our catalog of both fiction and nonfiction titles, featuring authors who represent a wide array of genres, as well as our established, industry-wide reputation for innovative, creative, results-driven success in working with authors. SparkPress, a BookSparks imprint, is a division of SparkPoint Studio, LLC.

To learn more, visit us at sparkpointstudio.com.

CPSIA information can be obtained at www.ICGtesting.com
Printed in the USA
BVOW05s1647030515

398756BV00004B/113/P